12 12 09.

Every Number
Is Lucky
To Someone

To Cathy —
Hope you enjoy
the trip...

Best

A Collection
Of Short Stories

By
Sean
Leary

every number is lucky to someone

This book is published in the United States by Dreams Reach Productions. The stories are fictional. Any use of real names in its stories, aside from those already cleared by the creator or those used in a satirical or humorous sense, is accidental and coincidental. All photos on the front cover are used by permission of the photographers and models.

Special thanks to Deanne, Bunnie, Robyn, Cayli, Jill, Ashley, Cleyella, Jeffrey, Shannon, Heather, Tristan, Kerry, Ross, William, all my MySpace friends and readers and everyone who has been helpful, supportive and positive along the way. I greatly appreciate each of you and, as always, wish you all the best.

As noted on the facing page, this book is dedicated to Donna Pesavento, my junior high literature teacher, who encouraged this budding juvenile delinquent to use his imagination for something other than getting into trouble. Thank you for being such a major part of my life.

ISBN # 0-9772819-2-2
Library of Congress Catalog Card Number: Applied for
First edition, October 13, 2006

To contact the author, e-mail seanleary@seanleary.com or ferris@qconline.com.

For more writing and information see www.seanleary.com and www.myspace.com/seanleary007.

To Donna Pesavento

every number is lucky to someone

Contents

every number is lucky to someone

Introduction

Disparate characters.

Going in different directions.

However, the occupants of these stories share a few tenuous strands. Some are looking to belong. Some seek healing. Some are trying to make sense of the oddities around them.

Most are consciously or unconsciously coming to grips with their own definitions of happiness in the face of society's expectations and the weight of their lives.

For some, this is a barely perceptible occupation and their efforts are hardly Herculean. Others have greater heartache or dissonance to conquer.

It's this variation and the perception by each of their own life's goals and obstacles that led to the title of this book.

Every number is lucky to someone.

Every situation is perceived and received differently by those in it.

And likely, every story will have a different impact on the reader to some degree.

I prefer to maintain that subjective response. I could inject my own intentions and interpretations of each story into this monologue. I could delve into the symbolism and hidden meanings of everything from the stories to their arrangement. But it seems more of a dialogue, an interaction, to me to allow you to come to your own conclusions without my intrusion.

I like the idea of the riddle's answer being left free to interpretation. I like that relationship between us, reader and author, sharing one very important thing -- a secret.

So I'll remain mum and just wish you a pleasant journey. Regardless of any greater rumination than that devoted to the narrative text, I hope you're pleased to meet these characters and enjoy spending time in their worlds.

Thanks for joining me there.

Best wishes,

Sean Leary

every number is lucky to someone

Winona Forever

The fat guy with the leather vest and nose ring is not happy with me. Neither is my girlfriend. They say I have commitment issues. They're right.

His flabby arms are a jigsaw of skulls, tribal patterns and devilish Bettie Pages that dance as he lightly stabs my girlfriend's back with an implement that looks like something Ming used to torture Flash Gordon. Orange ink starbursts are sprinkled around a pixie that will, she fears, make her self-conscious about wearing a strapless dress at her best friend's wedding in five months.

Still, she allows herself to leap forward. That's just one day, she says. This is forever. This is humid, fall nights at a bass-bounced club, awash in glitter- sweat and lusting glances. This is cool, early summers at the beach and looks over her shoulder, in the mirror, pretending she's a Coppertone model with a signature skin styling. This is afternoon sex, my fingers gently tracing the lines in the afterglow, kissing each kaleidoscope scraping along her shoulder blade and tracing the sweat down each firework with my lips.

But now, she's biting her lip trying to ignore the pain. He's flapping his lips trying to get me to join her.

``C'mon!" he implores, using patented junior high coercion. ``After a while, you won't even notice it."

Then why bother?

I tell him I can't make up my mind. I can't settle on one image, one symbol, which defines or inspires me to the point where I would want it attached for the rest of my life. Somehow, despite conventional wisdom being on my side, this is viewed as being a flaw, spattering me as a dismal failure in the exotic spontaneity sweepstakes.

However, I maintain, my capricious record speaks for itself. And not very well.

When I was a kid, I was sure that as soon as I was old enough, I would have Gene Simmons' KISS makeup tattooed onto my face. To my elementary school-aged, TV-stewed brain, that would make me the coolest person in the world.

Then I turned 10.

Gone was the desire for the KISS makeup, replaced by the realization that not even Gene Simmons had gone that far.

Next, I wanted the Van Halen symbol carved into my shoulder
--- another Machiavellian move in my plan for world awesome-
ness, along with the right buttons on my backwards baseball
cap, chrome valves for my Mag Scrambler wheels and, as a
lady-killing finish, radical bandannas wrapped at the bottom of
my ripped jeans.

My archetype for junior high domination lasted as long as
my crush on Lisa Bonet.

A parade of ideas for skin art followed in the ensuing
years of pseudo-maturity: A Notre Dame logo; a DePaul Blue
Demon; a Chicago Bear; a Chicago Bull; several JapAnimation
and Far Side denizens; more band symbols; a Calvin and
Hobbes; the Silver Surfer; Dream from The Sandman comic; a
village of tribal characters and enough
Chinese/Japanese/Sanskrit/etc. letters and characters to form an
alternate alphabet.

This is why I don't have a tattoo. Every couple years, if
that, the picture changes and I look back in relief that I'm not
branded with evidence of my own discarded passions. I can
talk about them or write about them, laughing in retrospect, but
ultimately I'm glad I'm not confronted with a ring of dancing
bears every time I get out of the shower.

My girlfriend brings up an ex who pierced my ear when I
was 15 and trying to impress. I still wear the diamond another
ex bought me, out of habit and look rather than sentiment. But
I could remove it and be healed in a few weeks. Removing a
tattoo would be exchanging a black mark for a scar.

Informed by an article in Cosmo, a college ex-girlfriend
once said my tattoo-less-ness was symbolic of my fear of per-
manence. I insisted it was more a practical acknowledgement

of my own periodic bad judgement. She concluded that my poor selection skills would result in me letting her leave. She was right.

She's twice-married with three kids of two fathers now, working at my aunt's bank as a loan officer. She tells my aunt that things are going great, and then proceeds to complain about whatever is bugging her that day.

Still, she's a respected member of her PTA. I'm sitting in a tattoo parlor, just shy of midnight on a Tuesday, wondering if the Chinese character for ``courage'' can, by mistake, end up smudged into the brand for ``stupidity.''

The illustrated man is finished with my girlfriend now, and she's fanning her hand over the new addition. Small beads of blood dot its lines, and she winces as he dabs them off with an alcohol-soaked cloth.

She continues to swipe cool air at her skin as the artist cleans his needles. She looks at me gleefully, golden-auburn eyes over a cute, cartoon ladybug smile.

``Do you like it?''

``Yeah!'' I return her buoyancy.

``Don't you think it's sexy?''

``Yeah, I do.'' I blow on the tattoo and kiss her back just to the right of it.

The tattooist's ashtray voice interrupts our potential Cinemax moment.

``You know, it's not too late for you to get one too "

I lean back in my chair. ``Ahhh, I think I'll pass."

She clicks her tongue and sighs. ``Oh, you're no fun."

I give the man my credit card to pay him for his handiwork. He swipes it through the machine, I ink my autograph
onto the carbon paper and we walk to my car.

``I think you would look good with one," she says, sliding
in the passenger side.

``Yeah, but which one?" I turn the key in the ignition.

``Well, that's for you to figure out," she says, fiddling
with the radio. ``I just hope you do it before you're eighty or
something, because then you'll really look stupid."

``What's the difference? If I get it earlier, I'll still have it
when I'm older."

``Yeah, I guess," she says, settling on a station. ``But
you'll miss out on being able to enjoy it when you're young."

I pause. ``I'm sure I'll get one eventually," I say, still not
100 percent, still mulling over my options hours later as I
leave her apartment, calculating how much sleep I can steal
before I absolutely, positively have to fall out of bed and get
ready for work.

When I get home, I remain undecided, yet amused by the
former ``certainties" of my past. But as I get ready to call it a
night, I can look in the mirror and I'm able to smile, in large

part because I don't have demonic KISS makeup staring back at me.

Still, all it takes is a few moments' concentration and I see them all --- the once-iconic reminders of interests faded. They each seem so real, such solid emblems of those particular eras, and for a moment it's amusing to imagine each of them and how they would have potentially translated to my life now.

However, the more thought devoted to them reveals the reasons why each is best left to nostalgia. So, in a blink, they're gone, left to the past, replaced by a personal statement of unclaimed flesh and open possibilities.

every number is lucky to someone

Whatever Gets You Through The Night

I was never a big fan of the Grateful Dead. Probably, as a side effect of that, I remember what happened on the day of Jerry Garcia's death. But to be honest, the only reason I remember it at all is because it's the first time I had ever seen my friend Riff cry.

Check that. It was the second. He also sobbed the day his cat, Marley, ate most of his stash. Tears budded on his cheeks as he ground his hair in his hands, chanting, "Oh, maaaan..." like a mantra. Meanwhile, Marley viciously ran in circles and chased mice ghosts around the apartment.

However, not even the sight of Marley getting caught in the curtains could cheer Riff up on his latter day of sorrow. The demise of his beloved Jerry caused a violent change in my former college dormmate and current neighbor, and it raised havoc in the lives of those floating about him like stained glass on a mobile --- those modern day Bedouins, the Deadheads.

The Deadheads (the hardcores, not the poseurs who have gone to three concerts, yet festoon their cars with bumper stickers like overactive teen girls with four fresh bedroom walls, a roll of tape and a stack of Tiger Beats) are the roving fans who shadowed the Dead from show to show, bartering for food, tickets, bootlegs, living materials and drugs.

They're tie-died anachronisms. Kids who missed the '60s and adults that wished the decade hadn't ended. Docile and friendly, they're charming throwbacks to a more hazy, innocent era. In those days, "The Man" may have called them vagrants and told them to get jobs, haircuts and lives. But now, in these more enlightened times, we simply stare, point and giggle at them.

Despite my lack of passion for the psychedelic music and leftover Twiggy Time culture that lit their lava lamps, I have maintained quite a few friendships with Deadheads based on their peace-loving demeanor, the quality of their personal character and the great parties they hold. Plus, many of them originated as fellow art majors before becoming Deadheads.

OK, actually, first they became college dropouts, then they became Deadheads.

Regardless, they were shattered by Jerry's passing. Well, by that and the fact that McDonald's started them out at barely seven bucks an hour.

As for Riff, whose income emanated from the financial remains of a dead grandma, his despondence was of a more singular nature. When Jerry died, his raison d'etre shriveled.

Shockingly, he was forced to take stock of his life. Sadly, the market crashed.

It took all the strength in my friend's rainbow-rag draped bosom, and practically half the harvest of his personal garden, to keep him from joining his idol.

The same could be said of his familiars. For two weeks, dreadlocked groupies swathed in peasants' clothing and patchouli slid in and out of Riff's, commiserating about their great loss while leeching off the resources of a corpse they had actually met.

The mourn-in made the street outside our apartment complex look like a used car lot for Volkswagen vans. Every morning as I left for work I was greeted by some ragamuffin remnant from a Life magazine "Woodstock" spread who had just made the long trip in from someplace undoubtedly much more exotic than this one. As I passed them I would scowl in my coffee, but by my noontime lunch of employee bitching and unfiltered down payments on lung cancer I would envy their adrift, seemingly   charmed lives.

When I returned from work, a rumpled shadow carrying nuked dinner in styrofoam, I found myself oddly buoyed by the growing number of maudlin poems and flowered pictures taped to Riff's door. At least I was getting paid for my suffering, although I can't say I pursued it with the same zeal.

Each night, meandering, labyrinthine guitar jams seeped non-stop from behind Riff's door, seemingly borne aloft by a thick smoke that defied wet toweling at the portal's foot and threatened to contact buzz anyone within a 50-foot radius.

Within a week, Mrs. Halpersome, living in the apartment and thus connected to the venting system, above Riff's, began to tell me about conversations she was having with her parakeet. Needless to say, it was an amusing sidelight to getting the mail. After all, I had no idea Poncho held such an intricate grasp of Jane Austen.

However, when she growled that the bird was getting to be "a mouthy little bastard," it was just disturbing.

Fortunately for her, the crew dissipated. Riff's purple-ink scrawled note on hemp paper imploring me to watch Marley was the only contact I had from him for a good four weeks.

Then the postcard arrived. The invitation yanking me into Riff's cultural undertow. The proclamation informing me that the future deity of his subculture had been found, plopped on his ass next to Mary Hart.

Ladies and gentlemen, I have three words for you: Tour de Tesh.

Yes. Do not attempt to adjust the horizontal hold of fear on your faces. I'm talking about John Tesh, the rigor-mortised keyboardist best known for his Muzak-inspired instrumental and the Ken Doll/Frankenstein monster-like good looks displayed on "Entertainment Tonight."

This, I had to see.

I'm sure Poncho would have agreed.

Using a long weekend to join Riff and his peripatetic pals on their peregrination, I grabbed a front row seat for the brain-cell carnage at a concert in Malibu. When I arrived, Riff gave me a drink that I probably didn't want to know the contents of, and a quick recap of the situation that was likely more frightening than whatever was quickly corroding my tongue.

The movement had begun a few months earlier, even before Garcia fizzed, when Tesh's oh-so-cheekily titled "Sax on the Beach" hit No. 1 on the Billboard New Age album chart. That Tesh's move shoved his phenomenon elevator to the top floor of zeitgeist enterprises was surprising. After all, we all know how much clout being No. 1 on the New Age charts carries. It's kind of like being the best surfer in Omaha.

But for some reason --- and I'm not discounting witchcraft here --- Tesh began gaining fans with an exponential growth matching the number of baby boomers claiming to have been at Woodstock in the years following it.

After Garcia's death, Jer's groovy ronins needed another hero to worship, and perhaps another reason to avoid reality. You can never have too many of those.

Enter the Tesh.

"It all started when a Tesh concert was aired on PBS right after a Dead gig," Riff purred. "People got a taste, and they got hooked. The sights, the sounds... the tunes got the trippy flow, bro!"

It seemed unbelievable that Tesh would be the next messiah of the hippie culture; that his gigs had become the hedonistic mini-malls Dead shows had grown to be. But after hooking up with the Teshheads, I saw the light rock.

Stunningly, the Rit-stained throng were now devoted to Tesh. Noshing on espresso bean burritos, decrying bad Mannheim Steamroller, distributing PBS leaflets and wearing bandannas braided with dancing skeletons topped by the face of Connie Selleca, the Teshheads were a placid, comforting, familiar lot.

The styles had changed a bit. Men took to wearing cray-ola-box-colored sportcoats and turtlenecks. Women inked their hair jet black and bartered bootlegged episodes of "Hotel" in hopes of studying the Wife of Tesh. But all in all, it was the same gift in different wrapping paper.

Spinning dancers, nitrous oxide-packed balloons and tribes of mind-bent dudes blipping on tiny Casio keyboards along with the music speckled the congregation. As bodies swayed, Tesh clunked around the stage in a metallic Armani suit, shaking his silver booty from keyboard rack to keyboard rack, prompting wails from fans in need of smelling salts and / or a good slap in the face.

"New Age! New Agggggeeee!"

"Tour de Tesh! Tour de Tesh!"

"He's sweating! I think he's sweating!"

My friends were ecstatic. John Tesh, synthesizer god , was in the house, taking off on another spirited keyboard jam.

"He never plays the same set from night to night," one afi-cionado giggled. "Of course, we wouldn't know if he did any-way, because we're all bombed out of our gourds."

As only I wished I could've been. However, despite my valiant efforts to speedily get there, oblivion didn't arrive fast enough.

My buddies were still stoked five hours later, as we drove on in their van, maps marked to the next gig, feasting on Ben and Jerry's Toasty Tesh ice cream.

"Tesh is the man, man," Starshine slurred as toasted almonds glazed with white chocolate in a vanilla ice cream base ran roughshod through the maze of hair in his sweetly trimmed goatee. "I wasn't sure of it myself until I had a dream. It had to be a sign. I was surrounded by Tesh's music when Garcia appeared to me in a heavenly light, telling me to get out and follow Tesh.

"Well, at least I think it was a dream. I could've passed out in an elevator and a fat, bearded maintenance guy could've woken me up and told me to get lost."

The others nodded blankly.

"I just needed release --- my life was so barren, I was a lonely vase waiting for beautiful flowers," Rhiannon aired in a wan voice that made Goldie Hawn sound like Bea Arthur.

"I had to get out of the rat race --- serving up all that fried corporate food brought me down," Daffodil added. "I could feel the bad karma building up inside of me. And plus, D'Arcy was always hogging the headset on Drive-Thru."

In the background, another great dead man, John Lennon, whined on the radio. "Whatever gets you through the night...baby it's alright, baby it's alright..."

The old speakers weren't very cooperative and he sounded trapped in the dashboard. The volume rose to accompany the positive reinforcement from those in earshot. I wondered if any Lennon fans drifted over to Christopher Cross in 1981 as I finished the remains of my eco-friendly ice cream.

"God, I'm not a very religious man," I thought, "but I promise I'll try very hard to mend my ways if you see it in your will that nobody starts..."

Darla began crooning along.

Daffodil tapped the bongos.

I contemplated jumping out of the van.

Whatever gets you through the night, I pondered, knowing that the only thing that would get me through this night was a strong sedative and the promise of a bus ticket home the next day.

every number is lucky to someone

Transubstantiation

I could tell it was a holy day. My Dad couldn't stop saying the name of the Lord on our way to church. Not in the way God would've liked, I assume, but repetition had to count for something.

``Goddamn it! Goddamn it! Goddamn it!"

This morning, he went out to retrieve the paper and returned with a bad mood.

``Goddamn it! Goddamn it! Goddamn it! Elise!"

Elise was my Mom. Not his pet name for God.

Slamming and shouting ensued, followed by my Dad storming outside in jeans, t-shirt and baseball cap. My brother and I watched as

---

he skulked towards his navy blue Buick and tore open the trunk, yanking tools out and throwing them to the gravel driveway. This was followed by a trip to the garage and dusty, forsaken tires being dragged out and chucked next to the sunken car.

The prelude to this tragic event happened yesterday, when a group of long-haired teens had wandered a little too slowly -- for my father's preference -- through the alley behind our house.

``Goddamn hippie shitheads...'' my father groused under his breath as he chopped away at our unruly bushes. ``Probably casing out the place. Lazy, no-good bastards...''

Usually he only pulled out the big guns of obscenity for knock-down, drag-out fights with my Mom, or for when he was really mad at me or one of my brothers and sisters. But not today. It was a special occasion.

``Fuckin' scumbag kids...''

I hate to say it, but it was his own fault. He started it. At the time they hadn't really been doing anything but leisurely walking and laughing, playfully pushing each other around. Why he decided to do anything was beyond me.

Besides, did he really know who he was dealing with? These were the dissonant drifters from the outskirts of our neighborhood, a pack of high school wild boys so dangerous they dared to attempt to grow mustaches.

Periodically, they would shuffle through the broken pavement pathway behind our home. Where were they headed? I don't know. I never got up the courage to follow them to find out. But most likely it was to wherever the cool kids went.

My mind jagged with possibilities. It was probably some improbably awesome Quik Stop. There, tattooed rock chicks with pale skin, blackened hair and dangerous eyes put out big time, serenaded by the roar of idling engines. Led Zeppelin and Slayer screamed from a boom box behind the counter, and if anyone didn't like it -- but most of the people did because everyone who went there was so cool -- then they knew where to go. That's right. Hell. And the clerks, all former Hell's Angels and Metallica roadies, let the really awesome kids steal as much Gatorade as they wanted.

Yeah.

They were swathed in AC/DC and Ozzy Osbourne t-shirts no doubt as black as their hearts. Skin-tight, ripped, oily jeans painted to their legs, torn Chuck Taylor tennis shoes strapped to their feet, ragged hair cloaked the devious Clint Eastwood slants of their eyes and spilled defiantly past the collars of their thrift store army jackets. A chain gang of Marlboro smoke wraiths bullied the air in their wake. They were the four horse-men of the Hunter Street PTA's apocalypse, and if you looked just right in the midday sun, their shadows seemed to be per-manently giving the finger to anyone who would dare to cross their paths.

My friends and I would watch them from our treehouse in awe. Our second grade transgressions lagged far behind the high bar these rogues had set, no matter how many rulers had been broken over our heads by Sister Barb. We would study them, envying their power, waiting impatiently for the day when we could ignite such chaos.

The best we could muster was a secret gang called The Devils. Invitation only. Except for Steve's little brother, who threatened to tell on us after he caught us stealing a beer from their Dad's fridge in the garage.

The beer was part of our ritual. It was my idea. Each member, at least once a month, would have to take a can from his parents' fridge and bring it to our meeting. We would pass them around and take one sip from each, grimacing at the noxious brew. Then the most recently inducted member would have to dump them out over the side of our fortress and take the empties to the beat up plastic trash cans behind our neighbor's garage, four houses down, burying them under stinking, pregnant, as-yet-unclaimed bags to escape detection.

Only one of us had been caught stealing cans from our parents amply stocked refrigerators. Tim. Nabbed sneaking it back to his room by his older brother. To his credit, he didn't rat us out. To his brother's credit, he let it go, taking the beer from him and remaining silent in exchange for a month's allowance and clandestine servitude as a room cleaning service for that same month's span.

At the end of his time as a maid, Tim was shocked to find the same beer can, drained and crunched up, at the bottom of his brother's trash basket. But, true to his nature, he remained mum about the whole thing. Tim. The guy was a rock.

As we munched blackberries illegally pilfered from Mrs. Grant's yard down the street, knowing full well, but not caring a bit, that it would spoil our dinners, we speculated on whether or not the exchange of contraband fireworks pocketed last 4th of July would be enough to gain admittance into the cool kids' club. Just in case one of us would ever get up the nerve to raise the possibility, we always kept some on hand, squirreled away wrapped in a sheath of t-shirts, behind a pile of skateboarding magazines. Just in case. But it never happened.

Typically, we'd notice the horsemen slinking through the alley and we would remain frozen in our admiration, laughing as they flung spent cigarette butts into yards. Even if those yards were our own. Even if we knew we would be the ones forced to pick them up later.

It was during one of these moments that my father decided enough was enough. Whatever it was they were doing, he didn't like it, especially since whatever it was they were doing was much less strenuous than the yard work he'd been sweating his way through all day. As far as he was concerned, the horsemen were demons that needed to be exorcised, driven from our alley and into minimum wage jobs.

He said as much to them yesterday afternoon. With a half-finished can of Schlitz in one hand and a weed whacker in another, he erupted with the force of a hops-fueled Vesuvius. Their response to the farmer-tanned berzerker with the island woman and the odd letters tattooed on his arm was predictable, simple and silent. Disdain, represented by a flock of upturned birds. They didn't even bother to say anything to him. That was how cool they were. Their fingers did the talking.

But, unfortunately for us, that was only their response at the time. Apparently, long term, they had other plans, as the slashed tires seemed to prove.

``Goddamn it! Goddamn it! Goddamn it, Elise! Those Goddamn kids! I'm gonna kill 'em! I swear I'm gonna kill 'em the next time I see 'em!"

``You're not gonna kill 'em, Frank, calm down.''

``I'm gonna Goddamn kill those little shits!''

``Whatever.''

My Mother and I could hear him downstairs, smashing the screen door against its hinges, rampaging through the house. She sighed and rolled her eyes, continuing to wrestle with tying my tie in front of the floor-length mirror in their bedroom.

``Stop fidgeting,'' she said.

I tried to concentrate on anything but the noose closing around my neck. I scanned the room. The unmade bed, with its yellow and light green geometric patterned comforter strewn across it. The two dresses she'd considered before settling on the light violet one she wore. The massive oak dresser, its top higgledy piggledy with wallets and jewelry and spare change.

Old pictures framed and dusty above the scattered junk showed their history up to that point. Their wedding day. A family portrait. An ancient vacation, the two of them young and smiling on a beach. Grandparents. And a group of men in uniform, in some sort of barracks, palm trees in the background. Dad's teenaged face smooth and unfolded, his hair shorn and shiny.

I had asked him about that picture once.

``That was when your Dad was in the war.''

``War? Cool! What was that like? Was it like on TV and

stuff, like `The A-Team' and `Rambo.'"

He looked at me strangely. ``No, it's not like that at all."

And then he'd take another drink, and that's all he would say about that.

Drooping from a hanger looped over his open closet door, the dark blue of my father's suit was joined by a red tie similar to my own navy one. It was silk. Chunky. Pre-tied. It waved slightly in the current from the dull, yellow fan wedged into an open window. Aided by the artificial breeze, it threatened to soar free, only to be halted by the thick knot locking it looped around the neck of the hanger.

``Okay, you're finished," she said, pointing me in the direction of the mirror.

And there I was. A little angel. Or at least dressed like one. My good khaki pants. Brown leather shoes, freshly shined. My summer-tanned skin berry brown against the snow white of my starched dress shirt, buttoned to the top. Blond hair washed, brushed, parted to one side and shining. And a tie. The first I could remember. Resplendent with a shimmering gold cross pinned right in the middle.

It was my first communion day. The third sacrament of my life, after confession earlier that year and baptism when I was a baby. At the time I'd lie and tell people I had vague memories of my baptism, even though I was about three weeks old at the time.

``I swear I remember it," I said.

``You do realize that it's nearly impossible for a three-week-old baby to retain those memories?" Sister Barb would retort.

``Seriously, I'm not kidding, I remember," I said. ``The water was cold and the priest's breath smelled like an onion and cheese sandwich."

``Uh huh."

My Catholic school compatriots and I had been preparing for this day for months. Ever since entering the second grade, we'd been in training, trying to learn what this meant, trying to decipher what exactly it was that was going to bring about such a monumental change in our lives.

We'd already gone through confession, although that was pretty self-explanatory. You'd go into a booth, pull back a little window and tell the priest all the bad things you'd done. Most of mine involved stealing, including the aforementioned beers.

``So you have your friends steal beer for you too?"

``Yes, Father."

``But you don't drink this beer, do you?"

``Only a sip."

``Only? Are you sure?"

``Yeah, it tastes pretty gross, actually."

``I see."

``Is that a sin, drinking the beer?''

``Well, you shouldn't do it.''

``So it's a sin.''

``Er, yes. I suppose since it was linked with stealing, especially since it was linked with stealing, then it would be a venial sin.''

``A venial sin, not a mortal sin?''

The priest laughed. ``My son, I certainly hope you would not be committing any mortal sins. Those are some pretty serious actions.''

``Like murder, right?''

``Yes.''

``But only people, or animals, not like bugs or anything.''

``Yes.'' He chuckled.

``But not like stealing beer or drinking it.''

``No.''

Then he'd give you a ton of prayers to say and you'd go kneel in a pew for about a half hour and say them and that would be it. Your sins would be absolved. You'd be forgiven. Simple as that.

But communion was different. It was more than what it

seemed to be. Or at least that's what we learned.

``Communion is the sacrament where you take Jesus' body and blood inside you, so you have to be pure of mind, heart and spirit for that to happen," Sister Barb said.

``So we eat Jesus' flesh and blood?" Jamie chimed in, grossed out.

``No, it's like a little circle of bread and some wine," Chris countered.

``We get to drink wine!?! Cool!" Anthony perked up.

``No, we don't get wine, we get grape juice, like at Thanksgiving dinner," Sandy said. ``You can't give kids wine. My sister in high school can't even drink it. She and some of her friends got busted for having a party and they had some vodka from my parents..."

``Class, pay attention," Sister Barb interjected.

``So are we gonna get to drink wine?" Anthony asked.

``Yes, you are going to get to drink wine," she said. ``It's wine mixed with water..."

``Yyyyes!" Anthony raised his arms in triumph.

``But it's nothing more than a sip," she said, bursting his bubble. ``You get one sip of wine, and a communion wafer, which is like bread."

``So where does Jesus come in?" Chris asked.

``That's what we're going to learn about,'' she said. ``The bread and wine are transformed through a miracle of the holy spirit into the body and blood of our Lord Jesus Christ.''

``So it really is blood and skin and stuff?'' Sandy was grossed out.

``Yes, but it's not like that...''

``Cool!'' I jumped in. ``We're gonna be like zombies! Awesome!''

I started fake gnawing on my forearm. Sister Barb grabbed her yardstick and smacked it against the podium.

``Class! Pay attention! I will explain everything as we go along, but for now you are to be silent, listen to me and follow along in your books. Now! Thank you.''

Over time, and through several lessons, many of my questions were answered. But it still didn't make much sense.

It was bread and wine. But there was something like magic and it was also the body and blood of Jesus. At the same time.

I didn't know how a thing could be two things at the same time. Sister Barb said it was called ``transubstantiation,'' which was where something changed but it was also in the middle of changing so it could be two different things.

I still didn't really understand.

But it was fine. Everyone seemed to think it was a big

deal. I got to dress up and we all got to go to church and everyone made it out like it was my special day or something and then at the end of it all, I would get some cards and I would get to pick where we were going to go out to dinner. Although we weren't really going to go out to dinner, we were going to get takeout because that's what Dad said. So I picked Mr. Krispy Chicken because I really liked their chocolate parfaits and the barbeque chicken looked good too.

Thinking about it made me hungry. I hoped the communion thing didn't last too long.

``Mommy, Daddy's yelling again,'' my sister Melanie walked in, all ready to go in a daffodil dress and matching gold barrettes with butterflies on them.

``Yeah, I know,'' my Mother said. ``Are your brother and sister ready?''

``I think Diana is, but Jimmy's still in the shower.''

``Well, tell him to get his little butt moving. We've got to be there in a half-hour.''

My Mom need not have worried. My Dad, shirt pitted and puddled with sweat and face red and puffy, barged into the bathroom and herded my brother out, all the while griping ``there better Goddamn well be some hot water left...''

``Dumb-ass,'' my Mother said under her breath, before catching herself and looking at me. ``Don't tell him I said that.''

``Don't worry, I won't,'' I said, cherishing the fact that I now held an adult secret.

My father, true to his word, was in and out and ready to go in all of twenty minutes, combing his hair, yanking his tie up around his neck and splashing on some Old Spice. But while his outward appearance had changed, his demeanor hadn't. Driving slowly to the church on three balding extras and a small spare didn't help.

``We're gonna be late,'' I whispered to my brother.

``Josh says we're gonna be late!'' Jimmy squealed, oblivious.

I punched his arm. ``You dumb-ass!''

I paused, waiting for a correction. But my father was too busy unleashing a string of profanities to care that I had just opened the cage on one of my own.

At the behest of my mother, my father pulled up in front of the church to let me off, just in time. My class had already started to line up in alphabetical order, waiting to proceed inside and file into the seats of honor - the first four rows of pews.

``Dude, we're totally gonna get drunk on that wine,'' Anthony said from the row next to mine.

``No we're not, you dope,'' Sandy countered.

``I am, I don't know about you, but I am,'' he said, smiling.

A few minutes later, Sister Barb led us into the church and to our seats. As we walked towards the building, slowly, two by two, over the elaborate stone cuttings embedded into the path christening the entranceway, I looked up and squinted. It was a clear, gorgeous day and the sun left everything in high relief. Shadows were short and cut starkly beneath us as we walked lockstep.

I stared down at the polished marble path, watching as the shadows in front of me merged and disappeared underneath the dark expanse beneath the stern pillars and polished stone awning of the church. Just before it was my turn to lose my shadow, I paused for a moment, scanned the burning sky, wiped the sweat from my brow with a sleeve of white cotton and glanced down at the indigo doppelganger on the ground beneath me. A halo, stalled.

Smiling, I stepped forward into the cool darkness.

Looking down, the floor was a shady, uniform gray-blue tint.

The shadows were gone.

We shuttled into our rows and sat down, flipping disinterestedly through hymnals, chattering, waiting for the mass to commence. Once everyone was seated, the priest took his place at the fore of the expansive, white marble womb, raised his arms and turned his palms to the heavens. Solemnly, he began droning in a monotone that hypnotized me into daydreaming about what TV programs were on that evening and what I could get with my eagerly-awaited chicken dinner.

I wish I could relate any discernable details from the mass

before the ceremony, but I'm afraid I didn't pay much attention to them. To me it seemed like every other mass I'd attended, with the exception of a few times when the priest would acknowledge us, the ``new members'' in the first few rows. Then, the congregation would applaud, waking us from our stupor.

It wasn't until nearly the end that things deviated from the program. Just before communion was to be dispensed, we were asked to stand.

``As you know, we have a very special group with us today,'' Father Morse said. ``Our second grade students are going to be celebrating the sacrament of the Eucharist for the first time. This is not a step to be entered into lightly, as it is a major commitment to our church and a joyful event to be celebrated as we welcome them into our community of brothers and sisters in Christ.

``So I ask you to pray for them in their journey in our Catholic faith. Pray that the Lord our God and our savior, Jesus Christ, bestow upon them all the blessings inherent in such a gift, and help them to always remember that they walk in faith and travel with the Lord.''

I looked over at Anthony. He made a steering wheel motion with his hands and smiled. I tried not to laugh. Sister Barb shot eye daggers through his chest.

An organ began to play a slow, solemn tune and the priest motioned to Sister Barb, sitting in the front row, at the far right of the pew. She stood up and stepped into the aisle, ushering the first rows up to receive their body and blood of Christ. The congregation lightly buzzed with conversation. The organ wheezed from the speakers. The choirboys sang in the background. The whole place reeked of incense. It smelled kinda like my aunt's apartment whenever she said she had been ``tending to her Hawaiian elm trees.''

Being that I had a last name in the middle of the alphabet, I got to watch the others as they walked up and partook, taking careful note of what they did so I wouldn't make a mistake.

When it finally got to be my turn, I stood before the priest, and he lifted a small, thin, white, circular wafer out of the chalice. Holding it up in front of me, he said, ``body of Christ,'' to which I replied, ``Amen.''

Not particularly wanting to have him stick anything into my mouth, I opted for the somewhat riskier choice of taking the host myself. Creating a throne with my two hands, palms up and overlapping, as Sister had taught us in class, I raised them upwards and he gently placed the host in them. Moving my lower hand, my left, to pop it over completely into my right hand, I then grasped it with my left and put it into my mouth.

As I'd been told to do, I resisted the urge to chew it, instead allowing it to stick to my tongue to disintegrate.

Walking over to my left a few steps, I stood before a second priest, holding the chalice of wine.

``The blood of Christ,'' he said.

``Amen,'' I said.

He halfheartedly handed me the golden cup, making sure to retain some control over it while still allowing me to lift it to my mouth to get a sip. The wine tasted sweet when it touched my lips, but left a sour aftertaste, particularly when mingled with the host, which tasted kinda gross soaking up the wine.

The priest then took the cup back, wiped the rim where I had drank, and got it ready for the next person in line. I walked back around and took my place in the pew, kneeled down and looked ahead at the gigantic crucifix hung on the far wall of the altar.

For such a joyful celebration, Jesus didn't seem particularly happy. In fact, he looked the same way he looked on every other day -- pained, saddened, his blood-streaked face weary and whipped under a crown of thorns.

I always wondered why, if we loved Jesus so much, we pictured him in such a way. You would think we'd want a happier memory of his life. I mean, how many people keep a picture on hand of their grandmother strapped to her deathbed?

No, we usually have a nice, shiny gold frame holding a soft-focus black-and-white photo of her from her younger days, smiling and vibrant, ready to go dance to big band records and sneak gulps of bootleg gin with stylish rogues who look like Clark Gable.

So why not a better picture of Jesus? One of him curing the sick or bringing Lazarus back from the dead or sharing a joke with the disciples? Why all the suffering and pain?

Do we really think he'd be happy to see our churches if he returned? Would he really want the first thing he saw in his dark, incense-smelly house to be a reminder of his worst moment the last time he decided to visit our planet?

I checked out the statue of Joseph on the right hand side of the altar. His right hand lifted in blessing, his eyes heavy-lidded, cheeks sunken down to a barely smile. The candles spread out before him in red glasses supported struggling, bobbing flickers.

On the left of the altar was the far more comforting statue of Mary, holding Jesus as a baby. A calm, loving look on her porcelain-smooth face, the many folds of her light blue robe highlighted by the dancing flames of the dozens of candles arrayed in front and around her, she was hypnotic and soothing. I smiled.

When the entire congregation had gone through the line, the priest asked us to rise again, as full-fledged members of the church, at which point we got a standing ovation from the crowd behind us. It was the first time anyone had clapped for anything I'd done. Despite it being for such little effort, I was happy to take it.

After the priest gave his farewell and led the procession of clergymen and altar boys out of the church, we followed behind him, two-by-two, looking like miniature grooms and brides in training. The boys uniform in khaki pants, white shirts and navy ties, the girls in white dresses flush to the knees, white tights, shoes and tiaras.

Once outside, we milled around, waiting for our parents to catch up with us, and I watched as children were hugged and kissed, haircuts tousled and stroked.

``We're so proud of you, honey,'' my Mother knelt down

and held her arms out to embrace me, and while I still didn't really grasp what it was I did that was so impressive, I was grateful for the attention nonetheless.

My Dad, now decompressed, patted me on the shoulder proudly.

My brothers and sisters, pretty much oblivious as I was, squidged about and stared, waiting for the hoopla to die down so we could leave.

Piling into the car, we took our place in a line of autos leaking out of the parking lot towards the street. Inching up, my father gripped the steering wheel tightly and stewed with every jerk and halt.

Breaking out into flowing traffic, we passed the bungalows and white siding homes, the taverns and the competing churches and finally made our way to the Mr. Krispy Chicken restaurant on the main drag of our town.

``We're not going in?'' Jimmy asked as the car snaked around the back.

``Why bother?'' my father said. ``We can go through the drive-thru and go home. That way we don't have to buy drinks.''

All I cared about was the chocolate parfait and my barbequed chicken, so that was fine with me.

``Mrrwwwrowww orddrrr prrlllessee,'' the voice through the speaker squawked.

``What?'' my father said.

``Mrrrowwww orrddrr pllrrllleessee.''

``Just tell him what you want,'' my mother sighed.

``Fine,'' my father said, ``but I know he's going to get the damn thing wrong.''

My Dad was right about that. Despite clearly relaying our order, it took another ten minutes of negotiations at the window to make it accurate, bringing my father to an even keener boil.

He handed three bags to the back seat.

``I hope you enjoy that barbequed chicken,'' he said to me. ``It's about twice as much as it would've cost us to get a damn bucket of the regular kind.''

``Jesus Christ, Frank,'' my mother chided him.

We headed back to the house. Car silent the whole way.

Once home, we sped through a brief ceremony. All of us stationed around the dining room table, with me at the head opening the cards I had gotten in the mail from distant relatives.

``Cool! Five bucks!'' I said, adding my grandma's check to the tiny pile.

When I was finished, my Mom took the checks and cash, separated a five dollar bill to give to me for ``comic books or candy or whatever," and placed the rest in her purse, to deposit in my mysterious bank account. I had often heard about this stash, around holidays and my birthday, but had never seen evidence of it. On bad days at home I'd imagine running away, absconding with the millions undoubtedly squirreled away in there and moving someplace warm I'd seen on TV, where the neighbor girls were always cute and the problems were usually resolved in a half-hour.

Once she'd cleared the table, the food was spread out and served up to us on paper plates left over from my sister's birthday. My father loosened his tie and made his way to the kitchen to fix himself a drink. My mother and my younger sister got us glasses of pop while my older sister passed out utensils.

My brother Jimmy, opening his fritters, raised one into the air.

``The body of Mr. Krispy," he said, solemnly. ``Amen."

He placed the fritter in his mouth and chomped it.

``Tastes like chicken."

He laughed.

``That's sacreligious," our older sister Diana said, laying down a glass of pop next to him. ``Don't do that."

``Why not, it's just a corn fritter? I'm just kidding," he insisted. ``Geez...and it really does taste like chicken."

He took a drink of his pop.

``The blood of Mr. Cola, Amen." He laughed.

Our other sister, Melanie, smacked the back of his head.
``Diana said to cut it out, Jimmy!"

``Ow! Geez! I'm just kidding!"

In the meantime, in the kitchen, my parents had begun to quietly argue. Or at least they tried to be quiet as they argued. This was followed by the typical response of the older girls trying to ignore it, and Jimmy and me craning our necks for a better look and listen to the festivities.

``Looks like it's gonna be a big one," Jimmy said.

``What do you think it's about?" I said.

``Who knows?" he said, going back to his fritters. ``Maybe she didn't want to go to Mr. Krispy?"

The last time they had really gotten into a big one, last weekend, my Dad had called my mom ``Super Bitch." Jimmy and I still hadn't stopped laughing about that.

``Do you think he's calling her `Super Bitch?'" Jimmy said.

``Shut up, Jimmy, and eat your damn chicken," Diana snapped.

With a withering stare from her, I dug into my own meal, but after a few bites discovered it wasn't much to my liking. The sauce was delicious but the chicken was surprisingly cold. Not cold in the good way, of chicken left in the fridge overnight before a hot picnic. And not lukewarm in the way of a halfway decent Sunday buffet. But cold in the way of something not microwaved all the way through. Disgustingly warm on the outside and squishy and wet just beneath.

``This chicken's kinda gross,'' I said.

``Then just eat your sides and dessert,'' Diana snapped.

I did.

About midway through our meal, our parents emerged from the kitchen. My mother was scalding, my father was gulping down the remains of a tumbler of something dark.

Looking at the table, for some reason his stare fixated on my plate.

``Why didn't you eat your chicken?''

``It didn't taste good.''

``Didn't taste good? How the hell is chicken supposed to taste?''

``Uhhh, I, uh...''

What the heck was that supposed to mean? How IS chicken supposed to taste?

``...uh, like chicken?''

``Are you being a smart ass?''

``No.''

A deadly silence struck our table. Fear froze us. We knew this side of him. It wasn't good.

He walked toward me. I got up and out of the chair. Quickly. I backed away from him. He stopped where I had been sitting.

``Where are you going?''

``I don't know, uh, I gotta go to the bathroom.''

``No you're not.''

``Yeah, I gotta go to the bathroom.''

``Frank, leave him alone, for Chrissakes,'' my mother said, firmly, but keeping her distance.

``Fine.'' My father stampeded his words out. ``Fine. I'll leave him alone. I'll leave him alone. I'll Goddamn leave him alone. I'll leave him alone to waste his food. To waste food I spend my good Goddamn money on so he can leave it here on his plate. I'll leave him...''

``Oh, will you shut the hell up about the damn food?'' she stormed on him, waving her arm dismissively. ``It's fucking Mr. Krispy Chicken. It's not like you ordered him roast pheasant from the Taj Mahal or something.''

My father turned on her, whipping his arm upward and then halting in pain just as fast. In his shoulder, near the bone, remained a shard of metal from the war. Most of the time it didn't bother him. Most of the time.

He screamed and the children at the table jolted upright in their seats. A chill ran through me as he turned, his face terrible, his eyes bloodshot and glazed. Planted in the spot, quaking with anger, he looked for release. He found it on the table, slamming his fist down on it.

The force made the plates jump, jarring loose biscuits and fritters off their perches and flopping my half-eaten chicken onto the tablecloth. Growling through gritted teeth, he picked the pathetic breast up, spun on me and hurled it.

The chicken, still smacking with remaining barbeque sauce and splotched with ketchup from the plate, struck me dead center in the chest. A crimson chunk on white cotton and navy blue silk, it made a dull splotchy sound when it hit and stuck, still, on the material.

And stuck.

And stuck.

For a few seconds it clung to the fabric, suspended. A sticky, crimson mass tainting the pearly white expanse.

And then, as if in slow motion, with a gloopy, smacking sound, it tilted. At first a centimeter, then two, then three, away from my shirt. Then, finally, it squidged off and onto the floor with a thud, leaving behind an oddly-shaped mark on my torso.

Its saucy corpse planted on the carpet, I girded myself against a verbal whipping from my Dad. But instead...

...he began to laugh. Softly at first, but then, as my mother and siblings joined in, he erupted into peals of laughter, until he had to sit down to catch his breath.

When he did, he reached on to my jilted plate, grabbed an untouched drumstick and took a bite.

``Jesus Christ, this does taste like shit," he said, goosing even more laughter from the table.

Taking a deep breath, he slumped in the chair. The room deflated slowly, as we waited for the other shoe to drop, or, be thrown through the air.

But it didn't.

He looked down at his glass, at the mess surrounding it. He took another deep breath and examined the room, all of us silent, uncertain. He turned to me and I quickly looked away, down, but kept my head up enough to watch him for any sudden movements.

``I'm...sorry," he said.

My mother rubbed his back. My sisters and brother reassured him. I picked up the cruddy chicken and put it back on the table.

My father looked at his watch.

``You know, why don't we go someplace good for dinner? Diana, why don't you and your sister and brothers put this stuff in the refrigerator and let's go down to Alfano's."

He looked at me.

``But first," he started to laugh. ``Why don't you change your shirt."

The rare sound of laughter behind me, I bounded up the stairs to my room.

Doffing the stained garments, I tossed them into the hamper and looked through my drawers for my favorite shirt, a navy blue polo with white horizontal stripes that began thin at the top and gradually widened as they traveled to the bottom. A few seconds of looking and then I remembered where I had put it. I had hidden it in a spot that only I was aware of, so that my brother wouldn't borrow it, as he was wont to do.

After locking the bedroom door, I went into the closet. I pulled away the stack of shoeboxes on the far right side floor, looked back at the door and listened to make sure no one was lurking, then carefully lifted up three loose boards that covered a gap between the two levels of our house.

There, commingled with a handful of contraband including more leftover fireworks, underground comic books I'd snatched from my uncle, fart spray, x-ray specs, fake poop and hot pepper gum, was my shirt, freshly folded and laid across a cache of six full beers stolen in careful increments from the fridge downstairs.

Again, I looked behind me, irrationally, at the door, then back at my rabbit hole.

I measured roughly with my hand and figured two more cans, max, could fit inside. Then I calculated how long it would be until I would be able to smuggle them outside.

Friday. Friday afternoon. Dad at work. Mom and the girls at a dance recital. Jimmy away at baseball practice. Me, here with my aunt, whose back would be turned away watching ``General Hospital,'' giving me time to sneak a backpack out the back door.

Friday. Friday afternoon. I would take them, all at once, into the back yard to empty into the bushes behind the house. Take the empties to the trash cans behind the garage four houses down. Shove them under the week's detritus, there for Monday morning's pickup. Bury them down, down, where my father would never find them. Hide them deep in the dark, discarded with the other venial sins of our neighborhood, waiting to be forgotten, waiting to be forgiven.

every number is lucky to someone

In Search Of
Warm Fuzzies

``Donnie, you can spank Santa later! We've got to get grandma to a diaper-changing station or she's not going to have a very merry Christmas!''

``Man, you got me on that one,'' Scott said, shaking his head and smiling.

``That's amazing,'' Kirsten laughed.

``Yeah it is,'' Andrea added. ``You know, Simon, that's so choice I would've thought you had made it up, if it wasn't for Cathy overhearing the same thing.''

``Dude, I thought Darien had it won with `Look at the package on that elf,' but hey, you've got it in the bag,'' Scott said.

``All hail the quotemaster.''

When you're working the hell that is retail for Christmas, you find ways, however small, to ease your damnation. The quote contest was one of our ways, at Baxter Sommers department store, to do just that.

The contest was relatively simple. It began the day after Thanksgiving --- the official onset of the holiday shopping season. All employees were eligible. Each entrant ponied up five dollars and kept his or her ears open. The person who overheard the best single line between then and today, Christmas Eve, would take home the pot. The quotes could be serious, humorous or just plain strange, although I have to admit, the funny and odd usually ruled. Gallows humor, I suppose.

Of course, there was some honor involved. Theoretically, anyone could make up an outlandish entry to try to grab the gold.

That's where the three wiseasses came into the picture. Each year a trio of names was drawn from a hat and this season it was up to Andrea, Scott and Kirsten to judge which line was worthy --- and authentic --- in order to bestow the buckage.

``Here you go, Barstow, 360 smackers,'' Kirsten said with mock congratulatory glee. ``Try not to spend it all on Warm Fuzzies.''

``Uggggghhh,'' I replied with a deep and genuine disgust. ``Warm Fuzzies.''

Kirsten laughed.

Andrea raised an eyebrow.

``Hey, what's Simon got against Warm Fuzzies?''

``Don't even get me started,'' I said.

Just about everything was wrong with Warm Fuzzies. Warm Fuzzies were the latest cash cow, gotta-have-'em, marketing-up-the-wazoo Christmas craze. Newspapers and TV had been filled for the last two months with stories of rabid moron parents clawing at each other to get these ugly plush creatures into their mitts. Because Lord knows that if their kid was the only one without a Warm Fuzzie on Christmas day, he could forget about being invited to play any of the reindeer games in his neighborhood. And Mom and Dad could likewise count on being emotionally pistol-whipped from then on in for junior's deep psychological scars.

Never mind that overstock of last year's must-have toy item, Upscale Trixie, the Doll That Makes Barbie Look Like Trailer Trash, was currently occupying the ghetto of the clearance table. When Santa's moon-pie face rose on the year's horizon, you had to keep your eyes on the prize. And this year, the prizes were odious little stuffed toys that looked like muppet members of ZZTop.

There were four Warm Fuzzies in all, each with different day-glo fur and corresponding facial hair. One of them, Fuzzle, had glasses and looked a bit like Jerry Garcia. Another, Gasso, had buck teeth and crossed eyes. Wazir was rainbow colored and sported a top hat. Ziggy played guitar.

Baxter Sommers was ground central for the rush, with the biggest stock of Warm Fuzzies in the tri-state area. Everyone had been here searching for the damn things. As soon as we got a shipment in, the lines --- and the fights --- began. And all of us working that day had a front-row seat for the carnage.

When you watch a middle-aged woman in a ``Christmas is for sharing'' knit sweater scratch past a teeming throng of soccer moms to elbow her way over to a toy and hit a bypassing nun in the face in the process, something changes inside of you. And that something goes rancid when you further see the frost-haired lady run to a register with a beaming sigh of relief, oblivious to decking Sister Mary Elizabeth.

Post-fracas, Kirsten and I carried Sister upstairs to the employee lounge to have a lie down. And as we stepped into the elevator, we could hear ``Rockette Balboa'' in the background, demanding free gift wrapping because our store's hectic pace put her through so much stress. Warm fuzzies, indeed.

``So, what do you have against Warm Fuzzies?'' Andrea, who was working in housewares at the time, persisted. ``I love Warm Fuzzies! I would've bought all four if we could've put any more than one on hold. They're cute.''

``They are not cute,'' I replied. ``They look like flabby hippies in plush. Granted, they're not as ugly as those freakish Cabbage Patch Dolls, but they're still nothing but overhyped, overpriced stuffed animals that have been pumped up and promoted to make people feel an insane need to own them.

``Consumers have been brainwashed. They think that by buying this rag they'll somehow complete their spiritual journey through the season and attain a beautiful, giving bond with their children. It's all part of their fervent hope that their kids will someday become the first generation that doesn't identify with the song `Cat's in the Cradle.'

``The Warm Fuzzies promise that, with their shiny plastic eyes and their third-world stitched smiles, when in fact they're nothing but a vile reminder of how warped and polluted this once-holy season has become with the human waste of greed.''

``Simon, you really are the most cynical person I know,'' Andrea said. ``This is the season for giving. Parents just want to give kids what they want. It's called love, you know? Don't you have any faith in people?''

``Sorry sweetness, but my faith shattered the same day Sister Mary Elizabeth's knee did,'' I said.

``Ouch!'' Kirsten grimaced. ``That was not a pretty picture.''

``Ah, Simon's got a touch for the melodramatic,'' Scott said, leaning against the register bay. ``And he's also got...hey! A Warm Fuzzie hidden there under his register!''

``Oooh!'' Andrea shrieked. ``It's Ziggy! Can I have him?!''

``What are you doing with a Warm Fuzzie, Mr. Cynical?'' Kirsten said, eyes slanting.

``I'll bet he's selling him on eBay like I did,'' Scott said. ``I got 900 bucks for mine.''

``I am not selling him on eBay,'' I said, ``although that is tempting.

``No, this is a purchase with a purpose. I'm buying this

toy --- and remember, it IS a toy, it's not a stock option or the light of the world --- and I'm giving it to my 15-month-old niece for her to actually play with. I know it's a novel concept, but I think my greatest joy this year is going to be seeing her drooling and slapping her sticky fingers all over this puppy. It's quite appropriate, don't you think?"

``Dude, I can't believe you're throwing away a Warm Fuzzie like that," Scott said. ``Do you have any idea how many parties you could throw with the money you'd get from that thing?"

``Oh, I have a pretty good idea," I said. ``I've had a good idea for the past four weeks. During every shift I've put that thing down there to keep an eye on it. And I've had to listen to idiot parents try to buy it from me. You wouldn't believe the offers I've gotten. Some of them would make Madonna blush."

``Well, speaking of offers, it looks like you've got company," Kirsten said, pointing to a woman who had wandered into my department. ``And we should probably get back to our posts for the last-second rush. Always happens."

That's the way it was the last hour before closing. The first half-hour, 45 minutes were slow. Most everyone was done and the last place anyone wanted to be at 5:30 p.m. on December 24 was at the mall.

But that final 15 minutes was killer. That's when all the latecomers streaked in.

People who had just gotten off work.

People who had dragged their feet and were in vital need

of presents.

People who were bound and determined in that last scrap of time to grab up anything remotely gift-like and toss in on their credit card.

It didn't matter that less than 48 hours from now most of these gifts would be right back here where they started -- returned unwanted and exchanged for cash. It was the thought that counted.

``Hi,'' the well-dressed woman smiled, draping a few items over the counter. ``I'd like these. Gift boxes too, please.''

And so it went. Click click click, zoom the card, memorize the name, wrap wrap wrap. ``Thank you so much for shopping at Baxter Sommers, Ms. Ross! Merry Christmas!'' Boom. That was it.

But that wasn't it.

``Caitlin, c'mere honey. Caitlin? Where are you?'' A thirtysomething brunette with rock glass spectacles and heavy steps slowly approached my register, following a voice that had emanated from...it.

``But...mommy...''

There she was. All three feet of fresh blonde candy smell and pink and cartoon ponies, wrapped around my poor beleaguered Ziggy.

``Caitlin, c'mon dear.''

``But mommy, it's one of them! It's one of them!''

``Ohmigod...it IS one of them.'' Ms. Ross' attention had been snared. ``I didn't think there were any left in the entire city.''

Dollar signs branded in fire appeared in Ms. Ross' pupils. In the background, the pink little girl was actually crying. In a ``Lassie came home'' happy way, of course, but still, she was like a sponge being wrung.

Oh well, I thought, Ziggy had better get used to moist children. I turned back to the register.

That's when I saw the look on the ladies' faces. It was a look I knew all too well.

``I thought they were all sold out,'' the mother said.

``Well, they are, actually,'' I said, somewhat smugly. ``That's my personal stash. I kept one of them for myself...''

I waited for the sales pitches. This was going to be interesting. A last-minute auction that neither participant was going to win.

``I'll give you $400 for it!'' Ms. Ross exclaimed like a warning, glaring at the woman who had dared to wander into her territory.

``Now, wait a minute...'' the other woman said calmly.

``I'll give you $600!'' Ms. Ross jumped in.

The second woman held her hands out as if breaking a fall. ``Hold on a second, I'm not bidding on it."

Ms. Ross whipped her checkbook out and was looking at my nametag, scrawling. ``$750 young man. Here's the check. Or I can get cash! There's an ATM in the mall. I can be back in a couple minutes."

``Uh, I don't know..." I said, drawing the words out.

``Nonsense! $900 cash then."

I paused. Dramatic tension mixed with nothing better to do was taken as affirmation.

``OK, deal! I'll be back in a skosh." Ms. Ross snapped her checkbook, shot an eye-dagger at her would-be competition, smiled tightly and power-walked into the mall before I could even try to stop her.

``I'm sorry, sir, but you can go ahead and sell it to her if you want," the mother said. ``I can't afford that."

``But mom, this is the one we've been looking for!" Caitlin whined. ``This is the one Carly said! This is the one on her list!"

``I'm sorry honey, but we can't get him," the mother said in a soothing tone that was as relaxing as a hot poker in the kid's eye. Caitlin began crying again, only this time it was a ``Lassie just got ran over by a semi" wail.

This too, I had seen before, and I wasn't about to fall for it. The last time I did, I sold my first Ziggy for the $29.95 ticket price to a ``destitute'' girl who then turned to her mother and said, ``This makes four Ziggys for me now, right?''

``You know, I'm sorry, but people like you, and situations like this, just disgust me,'' the woman scowled, plucking her child up as the toy dropped from small hands. ``Caitlin and I have been looking all over town for the last month trying to find one of these and it's people like you who have stopped us every step of the way. I don't think I could begin to tell you how important this was to her, to us, to find one. I don't think you'd understand.''

``Oh, I think I understand.'' I rolled my eyes.

``No, I don't think you do!'' Caitlin erupted, taking me aback. ``I don't care about your stupid Ziggy. I think he's ugly!

``My sister is sick and if she doesn't get an operation she might die and we don't have all the money for the operation to make her well. THAT'S why we need Ziggy so we can sell him for money for Carly...'' she trailed off into sobs.

Her mother patted her back. I shifted a little.

``Is that true?'' I said, still suspicious.

``You actually think we would make something like that up? Geez, I feel sorry for you.'' Exhaling heavily, the woman used her free arm to open a wallet obese with pictures. One was of a weak-looking girl with a flickering smile and the unmistakable penguin nose and sharded hair of the woman before me. She was in a hospital bed, tubes and tape decorating her like a sad tinsel.

``Well, Mr. Cynical, what do you have to say now? Do you think I carry around pictures of sick little kids in my wallet on the off chance I need them as a negotiating ploy?

My gut said ``Yes, yes you do. You're a sad, pathetic example of humanity that would have that type of disgusting moral compass to denigrate your child's life by making her dress up in such a way just to get a damn plush toy. You're just like everyone else I've seen in here, all of you wallowing in your poisonous `Christmas joy.'''

But then, even surprising me, another, small voice began to pipe up, gently nudging it aside.

She fumbled the wallet back into her purse. ``You know, you really need to have more faith in people."

``Yeah," I replied. ``I've been told that."

At that point Ms. Ross returned, slapping her money down on the counter.

``Here you are, sir, $900 cash!"

I looked at the money, then at the two women --- one smug and smiling, one bobbing a sobbing kid on her shoulder. It wasn't a difficult decision to make.

``You know," I rubbed my chin, ``while you were gone, this other lady offered me $1,000 cash. That's a decent amount more than what you're giving me. I mean, I'd have to be an idiot not to..."

``I'll make it $1,100!" Ms. Ross chimed in with fury.

``$1,200!'' mom injected, catching on.

``$1,500...and that's my final offer. Cash.''

Caitlin's mom shrugged like a bad actor. ``I'm sorry, sweetheart,'' the woman said to her daughter.

Ms. Ross slammed her hand on the counter like a gavel. ``$1,500. We're agreed on that, right?''

I nodded.

``I want to shake your hand on it this time.'' She grasped my digits hard as if she was trying to punish me. ``Now, here's the $900. I'll be back in a few minutes with the other $600. But that's it. I'm not going any higher.''

``Okay, fine.''

``You think I should try to push her to two grand?'' I said the minute she turned the corner. Caitlin and her mother grinned.

As to allay suspicion, the pair went off to roam the store until closing time, after Ms. Ross had long gone. At that point they met me at my register to collect my contribution to Carly's Christmas fund, along with an extra $360 that came courtesy of Donnie's Santa fetish.

Both Caitlin and her mom were quite grateful for the gesture and I felt that even though my niece wasn't going to end up with her very own Warm Fuzzie to vomit upon, things worked out quite well.

``That's a pretty amazing story,'' Kirsten said later at the staff Christmas party, handing me a cup of egg nog and $325 in fives. ``I'd say that easily beats Brandon's tale about the guys in duck suits. I kinda thought he made that one up anyway.''

``And yours even has a moral to it,'' Scott said. ``Kind of like, `Thank God for greed!'''

``Oh, I don't know,'' I said. ``After all, manipulating someone's lust for material goods to achieve a greater good is hardly the thing of an `After School Special.' But I guess it's marginally better than `A `Baywatch' Christmas.' ''

``I'm impressed, Simon.'' Andrea gave me a dimpled smile. ``I never knew you had a heart.''

``Oh, I've always had one,'' I replied. ``It just isn't shaped like a Valentine's Day card.''

every number is lucky to someone

A Fine Day For Porkpie

"Oops...almost got it."

The little boy scrambled to retrieve the football wobbling on the floor, the footies in his blue flannel pajamas skittering on the carpet. Reaching around the rough, leather oval, he shotputted it across the room.

"Good throw, Aaron," the man said, catching it.

The almost-three-year-old smiled widely. Nick underhand tossed it, and just as he had taught him, Aaron brought his small arms together to cushion the ball's downward slope, then clutched it, struggling, to his chest. This time it did not drop.

"Good throw, Daddy," the boy beamed,

reflecting the pride shone upon him. He stepped back with verve and launched a pass unexpectedly high and fast.

Nick leaned and fell to grab it before it went beyond them. Like the boy, he made a special effort to snag every wobbly throw. The loose closet door behind Nick was closed, but the broken doorknob would offer little resistance to solid impact, and the packed boxes piled behind it were full of questions best left unopened.

Nick's eyes scanned the clock as he rose. Almost two hours beyond bedtime. He felt a twinge of guilt. He promised himself only 15 more minutes.

But Aaron was far from tired. It almost seemed as if he could tell, but how could he? They tried to hide it as best they could. But he probably felt; in the hugs lasting longer than usual, the moments more filled, the words carefully considered.

In the other room, his mother was soundly asleep. This would not be her last night with the boy.

However, Nick knew there would be no more like this -- for any of them. And so he savored every detail, trying to fit an infinite picture of his boy into a too-small space. Trying to insure he'd never forget a gesture, a sound.

He'd clap his hands when he laughed hard, especially when the mice tripped over each other in "Shrek." Sometimes he walked on his "tippy-toes," particularly if he had a cookie in his hand. Certain words he said were still slightly unformed, like "peese" and "duice."

The boy's biological father, the woman's ex-husband, had

left a week after the boy was born and was never heard from again. Upon returning home from the hospital after having Aaron, the woman placed the baby's medical bracelet in an antique box with her wedding ring.

Nick met them a few months later. They moved in with him a few months after that.

Nick remembered her asking, when they first met, if he could ever love this child as much as his own flesh and blood. With no frame of reference, he could say nothing but an optimistic ``yes.''

Now, he wondered if he would ever love any child as much as this boy.

As the ball floated between them, Nick rewound the last two-and-a-half years in his mind; trying to find signs, symptoms, something he could point to. When the crack began to form. Instead he found evidence he shouldn't have ignored, and countless memories of the one reason he chose to overlook it.

Ironic, that as her business trips grew longer, her calls less frequent, he seemed to relish more and more her time away, time left between the two "men of the house." Friday nights spent reading Dr. Seuss. Saturdays going to the park. Pushing grocery carts, making racing car sounds. "One and a highchair, please." Dusk being met by two darkening figures; a small one being pushed on a swing, the other reciting a letter of the alphabet with each nudge.

Nick never imagined that somewhere else, two other darkening figures would be greeting the night in a far less innocent fashion.

They hadn't been married. There was only talk that dwindled in intensity as the months flipped by, replaced, Nick thought, by a sense of security greater than ceremony. He trusted. Never suspected. Now he wondered how long it would be before he could ever be that trusting again.

"Daddy?"

Nick had held the ball in his hands too long. The boy rushed him, giggling, jumping on him and yelling. The man laughed, dropping the ball as the boy tried tickling him with small sausage fingers.

"Keep it down, buddy, Mommy's trying to sleep."

Nick held one arm around the boy, giving him little noogies on his head with the other.

"What's your name?"

"Aaron."

"How do you spell your name?"

"A-R-N."

"Noooo...A-A-R-O-N."

"No, A-R-N."

Aaron wiggled as Nick patted his head.

"We need to get a brush through there pal, you've got knots in your hair."

"No, Daddy, knots not in hair. Squirrels eat knots!"

The man chuckled, as he had the first time the boy said it.

"That's right, and you know, if you don't brush your hair, you might get hair-squirrels."

"I not get hair-squirrels."

"You just might. They're very rare, but they have been seen in these parts, and they can be quite tricky. They could zoom in and hide in your hair and you wouldn't even know it, until they started to build their nests in your ears. In fact, I think I see one...right...there!"

Nick jiggled a finger behind the boy's ear, throwing him into fits of laughter.

"Right...there!"

"Daaaaady! Stop!"

"Okay," Nick hugged Aaron and kissed the top of his head, "I think I got 'em all out."

Aaron put his hand in his hair. "There no hair-squirrels, Daddy."

Nick sighed. He shifted the conversation topic to bedtime, as much as he dreaded it.

He knew that when Aaron left in the morning, he wouldn't be picking him up that evening, or any one afterward. That night, Aaron would be driven to a new life, and Nick wondered

how long it would be before Aaron understood that he would-
n't be going home.

Nick was unsure how many more times he would see him,
if any. Offhand comments his mother had made about the
uncertainty of their future hung steady in Nick's mind like
buoys. Subtle threats in ``negotiation'' for televisions and furniture made him realize he had, however cruel it seemed,
invested in a mirage. Without any blood tie he had no legal
rights and however integral his relationship with the boy had
been to this point, it was as ephemeral as the memory of an
infant.

The mark left on Nick wasn't so easily dissolved and it
wouldn't be soon healed.

The two walked to the bathroom to wash up, then headed
back to Aaron's room. Nick tucked him in. He kissed and
hugged him goodnight, twice, brushed the hair from the boy's
eyes and kissed his forehead again, trying to hold his tears.

Aaron looked up at him sadly. He could tell.

"I snuggle you?" Aaron held out his arms. "Snuggle you,
Daddy?"

"Okay, buddy." Nick laid down and Aaron rested his head
on the man's chest. For a long time there was silence.

"A-A-R-O-N," the boy whispered, and they both drifted to
sleep.

The next day when the man woke, the boxes, and the boy,
were gone. There was a quick note, about when she would be

back to collect the rest. By then the man would be at work, seeking distraction, activity. Anything but contemplation.

Two weeks later, the last phone call was made when she knew he wouldn't be home. Aaron was having a hard time, and she felt it best if there was finally a clean break. No more phone calls. No more visits. No more confusion over whether Aaron should call him "Daddy" or "Nick" when he told stories to the other kids in daycare.

Nick listened to the message seven times before finally erasing it, along with any thoughts of struggle. He loved the boy too much and realized the depth of its futility.

After erasing the messages, he stood motionless, his mind slowly draining, before taking a large gulp of air and pushing himself towards the back bedroom.

He found his pistol, loaded it, considered its weight in his hand.

When he returned it to its place, the handle was warm, the nose cold.

He sat in the boy's room. It smelled like an infant. Baby powder, ointment, stray candy, spills. He looked around at the bright starred wallpaper he pasted two years earlier.

His heart dropped. His pen followed. He began to write, stopping only to stretch, allowing himself to fall into it as deeply as possible, knowing that it would be that last time he could afford to do so for quite a while. Motion would replace feeling, blur it, to enable him to heal. The pictures he had tried so hard to capture would have to fade.

Five hours later he would go to an office and place a thick envelope in a metal safe deposit box that would remain as static, as steadfast, as the fidelity expressed inside.

And as he walked out he imagined, fifteen years later, a boy with an old football on a shelf in his room, receiving an unexpected package for his eighteenth birthday. He would open it to find a key and a brief note.

On the Friday before he'd leave for college he would drive half a day to the city where he was born. On marbled steps, Aaron would read from a yellowed envelope.

"When I first saw you, you were asleep. A beautiful, gentle boy with chubby cheeks that bobbed with your incredibly loud snores. They made me smile, and when I leaned over to brush a hair aside your forehead, the hall light framed your face and left me a mental picture I would carry with me forever.

``A portrait of my little boy. My 'porkpie.'

"This is everything I remember about you. Everything you were, and always will be, to me, and everything I hope you still are, to yourself..."

every number is lucky to someone

Getting Out Alive

They were seconds away from slipping into the shadows when the light slammed into their backs, freezing them, shocked and soaked on the rain-slicked pavement.

Jett knew, even before the bullhorned voice blared into the post-midnight air, that it was the cops, and they were busted.

He remembered this scene from countless TV shows, but now it was hard to do what he had fantasized about so often before. A small voice of reason inside him wanted to turn around and surrender. Throwing himself on the mercy of the voice. Handing over their pilfered street signs. And hoping that within a half hour he would be home, warm and dry, in bed with a ticket, a small fine and a great story for the morning.

``Shit, Jett, what are we gonna do?'' Archer asked, voice thick with excitement. Jett wanted to run, to escape daringly. But he was unsure if he was up to it without vomiting profusely, or if Archer would follow.

Jett bit his lip. Behind them, the voice pushed hard again. ``Come on boys, we saw you do it. Let's make this easy on all of us.''

``Fuck it,'' Jett grumbled. ``Run!''

Jett tore through the grassy ravine and into the street beyond it, his lanky surfer's body gulping ground with huge strides. Archer's stocky form ripped up the turf not far behind. Under their arms they grasped balky metal rectangles that slapped against their sides. The evening's goal. The adventure's take. Or so they hoped.

The police car was stuck within the confines of the parking lot, and would take at least a few seconds to turn itself around and pull out after them. Seconds Jett hoped would allow them to find a hiding place in the bushes along the fence that wound around the stadium across the street. Archer followed, old Nike shoes soaked, pounding along the slick pavement with squishy thuds.

Jett's heart felt like a machine gun throttling in his chest, yet no fear entered his mind. Only an invigorating sense of discovery, as if fleeing the police was part of a ``to do'' checklist of things he wanted to accomplish before he died.

There was a short shock of fear which quickened his step,

but it was more a token emotion, stomach-turning on a thrill-ride, than a full blown terror. Jett giggled maniacally as he ran just ahead of his college dormmate. This was a game to him, one he had been playing since he was a child, and his laugh clumsily tripped out of his mouth between short jokes meant to lighten the moment.

Archer, however, was of a different temperament. He was genuinely afraid of getting caught. Given time to stop and think, logic would dictate that he would be fine, even if they didn't escape. But logic took a back seat to the welling dread that this would somehow impact his graduation in three weeks.

Five years of college thrown away. Or at least the chance to attend the ceremony somehow rescinded. Of course they couldn't deny him his degree, but what would his parents think if he was refused the chance to march with his class, cap and gown shimmering on a sunny Saturday, to shake the hand of the chancellor and dean, and collect his blank piece of paper that said ``Congratulations! Your diploma will be mailed to you by July 1 after final grades have been officially compiled.''

Across the street, down a driveway and through a field outside the thick concrete arena there was a thicket of trees that enclosed the soccer field, lined on one side by a metal fence. Sliding away from the line of street lamps standing sentinel outside the football arena, finally, the pair were grabbed by the darkness. The branches of the pine trees around the stadium seemed to yank them into hiding, like molls slipping gangsters into a secret room in a saloon, behind a liquor cabinet.

They knelt down in the muddy ground, panting like dogs, glances darting out into the streets. Jett started to guffaw again.

``What the hell are you laughing at? What is so fuckin' funny?'' Archer snapped his dark eyes flat and serious and rubbed the rain out of his shaggy black hair.

``I keep remembering this line in a book,'' Jett smiled. ``It was Jim Morrison's biography. What was that, `No One Here Gets Out Alive,' or something like that? Anyway, he was getting arrested for screwing some groupie or something backstage, and he was screaming at the cops.''

Jett ran his hand across his forehead, slicking his long blond hair back away from his face, then began to act out a scene between the Doors lead singer and an irate officer.

``The cop goes, `You're under arrest.' And Jim goes, `Eat it, pig!,' slapping his crotch with a cupped hand. `This is your last chance to come quietly!' the cop says. And Jim grabs his crotch again and says, `This is your last chance to eat it!'''

Jett laughed. ``I don't know, that line just keeps running through my head, cracking me up. `This is your last chance to eat it!'''

Jett laughed again. ``Sorry dude, that's just freakin' hilarious.''

``And then what happened next?'' Archer asked.

``What?''

``What happened next. To Morrison.''

``Oh, he got Maced.''

``That's one hell of a comforting story.''

``Oh, c'mon Archer. Shit, they're not gonna Mace us if they catch us. They probably won't even step out of the cars. All we gotta do is wait here and wait 'em out.''

``I guess so,'' Archer said, pulling his coat tight around his broad shoulders and shivering.

``You know Jim wouldn't let them take him, the Lizard King would get out of this one. The Lizard King would never get busted for a fuckin' street sign,'' the words poured out of Jett's mouth. ``No fuckin' way!''

``What the hell are you talking about?''

``I don't know,'' Jett smirked. ``I guess I'm just trying to lighten the mood.''

``Yeah. I guess.'' Archer perked up. ``No Parking. Give me a goddamn break. It's not like we stole a stop sign or something. I could see them getting mad about that. I mean, someone could get in an accident or get hurt or something. But geez, `No Parking?' And it's a friggin' university lot anyway. All `No Parking' signs are for is to give them a reason to give out tickets and to raise money for themselves.''

``Yeah, no shit!'' Jett added. ``I paid enough money to this college. I deserve this. You deserve this. Hell, this should be your graduation gift.''

``Uh huh.''

Jett continued, still feeling the buzz of several dozen plastic cups of keg beer, although the sound of his voice did little to assuage Archer. Rather, it began to annoy him. It wasn't so much what his friend was saying, or his idolatry of Jim Morrison, whose name he repeated several times, but in the fact that it was a constant reminder that Archer was in the situation he was in. A situation he, as a 22-year-old adult, probably shouldn't be in. He tried to talk himself out of it, he tried to kick back and enjoy the ride, as Jett was telling him to do, but he couldn't. His buzz starting to wear off, he felt like an ass. An immature ass.

He watched the rain dribble from the trees enclosing them. It seemed as if every drop caught just enough light from the stadium halogen to reveal their clandestine retreat. But it didn't. He knew it didn't. That was crazy.

Jett had stopped reciting Morrisonianic quotes and began to chortle to himself, muttering a reassuring profanity every few seconds, until he sat panting like a wounded animal, alone with his thoughts.

``Jesus, you need to stop smoking,'' Archer said as Jett coughed and grabbed to catch his breath.

``I think I'm catching something.''

``Might be syphilis. Stay away from me,'' Archer said, attempting to distract himself.

``Yeah, too bad I didn't stay away from your sister,'' Jett retorted, ``I might not have had that problem.''

``My sister's eight.''

``Maybe it was your Mom then?''

``You're a doofus. You can't do over a family insult joke.''

``Sure I can. Maybe it was like that traveling salesman joke with the farmer and the guy sleeps in the barn with three holes and one's the mom and the other's the daughter and the third one was a milking machine and he gets confused.''

``That doesn't make any sense. A milking machine gave you syphilis?''

``Well, everyone's heard the joke, that thing gets around.''

They both laughed. ``You're a sick man, Jettson,'' Archer smiled. ``You're a sick man...''

``I'm a drunk man,'' Jett belched. They laughed again.

Archer and Jett had hung out together for three years, but had really gotten to know each other well over the past year. This intensity was due in large part to the fact that Archer was in his last year of college and Jett would be heading into those same final semesters the following fall. Jett went to great lengths to provide entertainment for them under the pretense of ``making Archer's last year of school one he'll never forget, before he has to enter the rat race of the real world.''

Although usually it seemed like this was only an excuse for crazy things Jett would have done anyway.

But it didn't matter much to Archer. He really didn't care one way or another about the motivation because for the most part it worked. He enjoyed it. He enjoyed the distraction. It kept him from thinking about what was waiting for him.

Having done most of the heavy lifting on his degree in his first four years, his fifth was spent finishing up a few requirements for a bachelor's in marketing and coasting through a second minor, accounting, that joined his previously completed minor in finance. Most of his last semester had been spent trudging through classes waiting for the drunken weekends to begin. However, in the last few weeks, he had begun to realize the finality of his impending commencement, and felt cold to its touch.

What he was graduating into was uncertain. He saw himself only as a near-fully-functional machine for making money. Just a tweak here, an uptuning there and he would be set. Right? After all, wasn't that what he was here for in the first place? Isn't that what his parents, brothers, high school counselors, professors, the magazines, newspapers and every consumer who had an opinion had told him the purpose of college was?

``Without a college degree, you're never going to be able to support yourself," his father had said, flipping the newspaper to a Mercedes ad and smiling as it opened a road of dreams across the breakfast table.

But still, he was tentative. It seemed like a black hole to him. All he had known was the world of the educational system. He had little ambition to join the ranks of the white collar proletariat, inching his way up for 40 years, waiting to die or retire, whichever came first.

Staying in school had kept him young, at least in his own mind. He had done well in the profession of a student. He circumvented difficulty through whatever means possible. It was all a game, playing for vague merits given letters to signify them for lack of anything new or inventive.

The thought of entering this alien world that seemed to have little use for him sent him reeling back to youth, clutching his rebellion like a sword against the enemy -- his fear of growing up.

He knew that sooner or later he would graduate and would have to surrender, but he blocked that from his mind with all the stubborn ferocity of a terrible two-year-old. However, the voice had visited him more often in the past few weeks, and on this, the final ``free'' weekend before he entered pre-finals week, finals week and the inevitable trudge to graduation, it seemed to shriek like fingernails on a chalkboard.

Just as he felt it ready to overcome him, his anger took over. There was an intensity in it that could not be denied, that seduced Archer into a feeling of fantastic immortality. No. He would not let go of college, his youth, this easy. He would not be compared to his brother John, who hit commencement in three-and-a-half years at the top of his class.

He had seen through his doe brown, 11-year-old eyes, John come home a mass of red, near-tearing jelly only months after he began his brilliant future. John had been fired from his perfect job -- laid off, technically. It was a cruel job market at the time. His new model-worthy wife left him after four months off became six, and six became a part-time job bartending, which became too many late nights and early mornings rolling home.

Maybe it was because he had never taken time to just

cruise when he had the chance, Archer thought. And so when he entered college, he was determined to take a more leisurely route, one of slow certainty rather than impatient determination.

But as the time grew near for him to face his final academic curtain, all he could remember was the summer after his brother had moved home, broke and alone and living in the basement. John's muffled sobs sneaking through the vent and breaking the dialogue of his cartoons. Him feeling uncomfortable not knowing what to do to ease his brother's pain.

He carried those sobs with him throughout high school, into John's rehab, and on into college, when John had become one of those incredibly happy people wearing cardigan sweaters, working with crack addicts and mentioning Jesus in pretty much every conversation.

John's transformation had caused Archer to discount him as an anomaly. But still, as Archer's own time approached, his brother's distant sobs exploded deeper in his mind each night before he finally fell asleep, their echoes growing louder every day.

``Think they're still out there?'' Jett broke Archer's train of thought.

``I don't know,'' Archer replied. ``But I think we should wait it out a little while longer. Just to be sure.''

Jett tapped his hand lightly and insistently against his sign splayed on the ground, face down to keep the reflectors from catching light.

---

every number is lucky to someone

``Ohhh, this is boring...'' Jett said, cracking his knuckles.

To Jett, college had been a soap operatic blend of relationships, altered states of consciousness and a dictionary of various imaginative props to check his time. The business classes he took for his parents and passed with ``no less than a `C,''' were nothing but his ticket to the amusement park.

On the particular night in question, the rides included two kegs of Rhinelander, ``the cheapest buzz around,'' a blasting stereo and a room filled with inebriated, sweaty people. This was followed by a makeout session with the cute cinnamon girl with the short amber hair that he'd seen several times in the cafeteria but lacked the liquid courage to approach. Then, finally, the debauchery was put to a halt by a third warning from the Resident Assistants making their rounds and clamping down on quiet hours.

Still buzzing, he and a handful of people, including the cinnamon girl now known as Donna, her blonde friend Claudia, Archer, Archer's roommate Jeff and two other girls, Trina and Ember, who kept pestering them to order pizza, consigned themselves to a chilldown of watching TV and trying to eat enough to avoid a raging hangover the next day.

That's when...

``You know what this room really needs?'' Donna chirped. ``Street signs.''

``Really?'' Jett raised an eyebrow.

``Yeah, you guys have pretty much everything else, but no street signs. I'm kinda surprised.''

``That sounds like a challenge,'' Jett shot a glance at Archer and the other three, who quickly bagged out.

Two beers and four shots of Tequila later, ``Butch and Sundance'' grabbed a bag of Doritos, two umbrellas and Trina's ratchet set and headed out into the wet sheets of rain pelting Dorchester at 3 a.m.

The storm was only a distraction to the two ``rock and roll ninjas on a mission from God.'' They cruised the campus looking for cool street signs, but when they couldn't get any off their hinges, they had to settle for two bright ``No Parking'' signs in front of the Math building. The first came off easily, but the second was evidently stuck to the pole with some kind of NASA super glue.

With a final jerk, after at least five minutes, it cracked away from its hinges and into their arms.

Ebullient in their triumph, they were oblivious to the car pulling up behind them. A Caprice Classic shark gliding through the water towards unsuspecting swimmers.

``Okay guys, drop the signs...''

``Okay guys, drop the signs,'' Jett mimicked in a goofy voice.

``I can't believe they caught us,'' Archer said.

``They didn't, yet,'' Jett countered. ``And they're not going to either.''

``Look at that,'' Archer pointed at the police car hovering

around the block, circling concentrically, pointing the spotlight out into the nooks and crannies of the stadium grounds.

``Shit! Down!"

The two of them face planted into the emerald grass. Both were wearing dark clothes, ``ninja attire" -- black cargo pants, black t-shirts and black jackets -- made all the darker by the rain that afforded them something of a cloak of invisibility if they could just stay cool.

Archer cursed himself. They should have picked signs that were more easily concealed, or ones which were located on some remote outpost of the campus, some realm far from the ones in a parking lot bathed in light that they had taken. Dumbasses.

``I think he's gone," Jett whispered.

``Keep your head down, dipshit!" Archer snapped.

After 15 minutes of slow torture and no sign of the police, they decided to venture out from their spot. The rain had stopped, but it had drenched them. Their clothes were heavy and cold. They carried their sins poorly. Underneath their jackets they concealed their treasures, red, black and white fluorescent sheets of metal.

Following the darkened trail behind the stadium and emerging through the gravel road on the other side of it, they found themselves within sight of their dorms at last. The trail was enclosed on all sides by a field of grass, flanked by pine trees, with considerable distance between them and the street to give them warning to any police ambush.

The walk divided itself into four distinct phases.

The first was tentative, as they wandered gingerly out from the foliage and onto the open grass.

The second was full of swagger and bravado, of feeling they were going to pull this off. They were Harry Houdinis! Brilliant! Masterminds! Escaping the trap of the dim-witted authorities because they were young, strong and clever! The police were old and fat, sipping coffee, eating donuts. They were stained green with jealousy of them! Their skills! Their tricks! Tricks those arbiters of rules in the adult world, in their clogged ways, could never hope to grasp.

The third phase was a combination of the two. An edgy intake of breath was brought on when they saw spectral lights which reached through the cocoon of trees surrounding them, permeating the wet grass near to the very heart of their path. They were smacked with doubt, with Murphy's law, that they were about to be caught, just running distance from home.

They began to rethink their strategy as the car lights approached from around the corner of the road in the distance, the pavement that acted almost as a moat between them and the towers where they lived.

Heads down they trudged on slowly, nervous as hell as the car approached. But it passed by, a small Toyota, obviously not policia. They exhaled as they veered back onto the gravel road that would lead to the bright towers before them.

They laughed and gave each other high-fives. They had completed the mission, the last great task of their college careers, and emerged unscathed. Walking with a brisk pace they closed to within a good 100 feet of the dorm doors when a pizza delivery truck sped away and revealed a badge-marked white van in the driveway loop outside the towers.

Their signs were hidden under their jackets, pressed close to their chests. They kept walking. They couldn't stop now. They were sure to blow it if they acted suspicious.

Nothing.

Silence.

``Whew, man that was close," Jett said softly as they hit the top of the steps and advanced on the doors to the dorm.

As if they had heard the last whispered phrase, the dark figures in the van called out to them to stop. They looked ahead and saw the security guards of the dorms approaching the other side of door, undoubtedly ready to search anyone who looked suspicious. Anyone like them.

``Fuck. FUCK!" Archer growled through gritted teeth. ``What the hell do we do now?"

``Turn around, turn around," Jett blathered. ``No, wait! Shit, I don't know. Damn. Walk, just walk, like we were just going towards the dorms, but decided not to. Try not to be con-spicuous."

``Yeah, great plan. Shit!" Archer gritted his teeth. ``We're fuckin' frozen. Surrounded!"

``Hey, you guys, didn't you hear us?! Hold it right there!" A cop got out of the van. The security guard from the dorms pushed through the door and walked towards them on the other side.

Jett looked sideways at Archer as they faced the field from which they had just emerged.

``Butch Cassidy and the Sundance Kid, huh?'' Jett said, kind of smiling.

``We're fucked either way,'' Archer said.

``Run!'' The soles of Jett's converse sneakers squeaked as he leapt into action.

They tore off aimlessly, in patterns like thrown dice, onto the gravel, into the grass. Each avenue they took into the previously empty field was now engulfed in a spotlight coming from the white van. Another police car roared around the corner. And another. Doors opened. Figures spread into the field. They were toast.

``Jesus, don't these guys have anything better to do?'' Archer complained, looking for a hole in the converging phalanx of patrolmen. By this time, they were enveloped in the field's soft grass, cut off from the dorms by approaching lights. They kept scrambling, but every direction they seemed to take was met with a slowly approaching car, dipping into the field like warships being set into the water, or a shadow moving toward them.

Jett kept running, but his circles closed in on each other and finally were halted altogether by a shank of authority from a bullhorned voice. ``Stop where you are!''

``Hold it!'' a man bellowed as his shoes whipped through the dewy grass. Archer turned just in time to duck and avoid the charging officer as the slick bottoms of the man's shoes sent him sliding to the ground. Jett squeezed out two seconds of laughter before being tackled to the mud by a second figure.

``Holy shit!'' Archer then felt his own world go horizontal as another flashlight-brandishing figure pushed his back and a thick leg kicked him down. His arms were pulled behind him as the cuffs were slapped on, stinging as the metal tightened around the skin about his wrists.

It felt almost hallucinatory, this strange event that was happening to him. The gravelly voice of authority spit upon him, whipping his back with words as a boot between his shoulder blades ground them in.

Finally, they were brought up, and allowed to walk to their individual cars of imprisonment. Archer took a last look at Jett, who was smiling through a clump of sod that had attached itself to the rowdy blonde hair above his left cheek.

``Come on, you asshole,'' the cop said, poking him towards the back seat of the car.

Jett laughed as he was shoved in.

Archer's only feeling was an impotent hatred. He loathed the men, the ebony figures that had run them into the ground. It was as if they were taking him away, forcing him out of his college fantasy and into the real world before he was ready to leave, before the show ended. And all for something so minute, so petty. A ``No Parking'' sign was only a device that allowed them to write tickets and take money. Money. It was all about the money.

``Bastards,'' he spit mud. He didn't want this to be the
finale, dragged away kicking and screaming from his stage,
from his props.

But now he had no choice. Enclosed by the fierce reality
of a steel cage in the back of a patrol car he surrendered.

He knew his future. His parents would bail him out the
next day, and two weeks later he would don his cap and gown
to take his place in the world whose road started in this slick,
stenchy back seat.

Enclosed behind a cross-hatching of iron bars, handcuffs
digging uncomfortably into his wrists, the car drove away, taking him to the station.

Archer's one phone call went to his roommate Jeff. It was
almost 6 a.m. when the pair were admitted to jail, given dry
orange jumpsuits and sandals and set in a holding cell with a
half dozen other drunken idiots, waiting to dry out literally and
chemically. A few hours later, they were marched out with the
group, a line of misfits, into court to the waiting disdain of a
tired judge. Punching them through with fines, court costs and
probation, Jett and Archer were sent back to the jail to change
into their street clothes and met Jeff outside for a ride back to
the dorm.

``Are you sure you guys don't want me to take you to the
airport?'' Jeff smiled. ``You looked mighty cute in those orange
pajamas. I thought maybe you might want to join the Hare

Krishnas?"

Archer smiled. A fine. A ticket. Probation in a town he was never going to see again, or at least not until homecoming, starting two weeks from now. That was all. And a story that would still bring laughter years from now. Jett was right. Not in what he, or Archer, did, but in its lighter shade of gray on the grand scale of things.

On the way home as his clothes evaporated, so did his worries.

Archer's parents never did find out. Jett's parents did almost immediately. They, out of the blue, called that day and circumstances convinced Jett this would be the best time to drop the news.

By chance, Jett's younger brother had been arrested the same night before, for playing ``mailbox baseball'' with his friends. So aside from some guilt-laden comments about it being ``such a proud day'' for his mother, he got off pretty light.

Back in the dorms, the two outlaws collapsed and slept until dinner. At 6:40, twenty minutes before the last meal of the day in the cafeteria was going to be shut down, Jeff woke them up to trudge downstairs. As they were entering the elevator, Trina was walking out.

``Where's my ratchet set, you douchebags? My uncle gave me that ratchet set! You fuckers better not have lost it.''

Jett turned on her.

``Eat it pig!'' he growled, slapping his crotch with a cupped hand.

Her jaw dropped, silent. The door closed.

Archer couldn't help but smile. Jett smirked in return.

Jeff laughed. ``Hey, what book is that from?''

Archer pressed the button again as the elevator began gliding downward, then turned back to him.

``No One Here Gets Out Alive.''

every number is lucky to someone

This Is A Call

The rug the Pope puked and pissed on lies on my porch, cleaned of everything but the memories.

Of course, its defiler wasn't the Pope then; he was only my roommate.

I was awakened with news of his promotion early on Martin Luther King Day. Too early. Mistri. She was the only one who would dare to call before noon on a day off.

"Lambchop! What are you doing?"

"I was holding a full house and had Jennifer Aniston down to a Wonder Bra."

"Riiiiight."

"Can this wait? It's MLK. A holiday? I'd like to get back to sleep so I too could have a dream."

"Did you see 'Reformation' last night?"

Forget it. She's hopeless. Especially when she wants to talk bad TV.

"Reformation" was one of our new favorites, a cross between "One Life to Live," "Goodfellas" and "The DaVinci Code." The church hated it, but viewers loved it. After all , where else could you see a trio of ninja nuns, who looked like swimsuit models, vacationing in Ibiza, while clandestinely on the prowl for the Spear of Destiny?

"No, I taped it," I yawned.

"Dude, fasten your seat belt. Moochie is the new Pope."

"Huh?"

"Moochie. Michael Mancuso. Your college roommate, my ex-whatever, is the new Pope on 'Reformation.'"

"You're kidding."

"No! A man we've both seen naked is now the most pow-erful man in the church. Well, the fake church anyway. Still, do you think that makes us sinners or something?"

"You maybe. I never slept with him."

"As far as you can remember."

She was joking, but in the unfocused kaleidoscope of that drugged, drunken, debauched time, who really knew for sure?

The first words Moochie said to me, the inaugural day of freshman orientation, as he walked into our antiseptic dorm room, were, "So, you wanna get high, or what?"

For the next two years of our lives, there was plenty of getting high and "or what." He was a drama major. I was a design major. A vast portion of our hazy days was spent "suffering for our art." This incredible sacrifice included recycling beer cans, selling plasma and soaking our parents (hence, "Moochie") to buy cheap booze and drugs.

That enabled us to conduct "chemistry experiments" -- parties enticing female art and drama majors into affairs that would give us all a rich well of existential grist for our budding masterworks. And, also, plenty of orgasms.

Both of us thought we were going to be incredibly famous some day. Everyone does when he or she is 19. In our demented little heads, where gray cells struggled in vain against a thickening horde of chemicals, we were slowly assembling our back stories to the legends we would become.

So, when Moochie drunkenly urinated on himself and the floor as several goth girls fell down laughing, somehow prompting him to croon "Waterloo" by ABBA, it was chalked up to a "Keith Richards moment" rather than simple incontinence.

Mistri was sucked into our black hole sophomore year, just after that first of many infamous rug incidents. She lived across the hall. Moochie met her late one night, while shambling to the drinking fountain, wearing only boxers. He was looking to fill a bucket for the waterslide we had built in our room, using duct tape, pillows and Hefty garbage bags. Three co-eds whose names I cannot remember but whose skimpy bras and panties are indelibly etched in my mind, were eagerly awaiting their turns on our homemade Wacky Waters set.

Aside from Moochie's quest for agua prompting his departure, he also wanted to find a place to vomit that wouldn't leave our room stinking any worse than it already did. False alarm, but I think he was impressed that Mistri stood around waiting even as he dry-heaved over the fountain. It turned out she was just bored and curious as to whether or not he was going to go through with it.

"Is there some reason you're not wearing pants?" Mistri chuckled.

"They were too tight," Mooch smirked. "I couldn't figure out whether it was because of my large wallet or my extra-large penis."

"It's probably because your ass is getting fat," she sneered, pushing him out of the way to get to the fountain before he actually did emit something rank into it.

The next day, we became better acquainted with her in the cafeteria during dinner/breakfast. She was looking for distractions and adventures, which were our specialty.

By fall break, we had corrupted that sweet, strawberry-blonde haired nymphette. Soon our disease had also spread to her friends, the recovering private school girls with whom she filled life by alternately emulating and living vicariously through Sylvia Plath, Jewel, and the cast of "Melrose Place." Good times.

Judging from the fuzzy memories and my squiggled journal entries, it was a gripping ride while it lasted. But before long, things began to sour. Grades sagged, sycophants and succubae flunked out, and, inevitably, boredom and inertia wedged Moochie, Mistri and me into a hellish love triangle.

Its surly unraveling led to a summer incommunicado between the three of us, and when junior year cracked open, Moochie was gone. Apparently, he mis-delivered two dozen pizzas to a friend's party, called his boss, Leonardi, to tell him to fuck off, grabbed a backpack and hopped a bus to Hollywood.

At first, Mistri and I gathered sordid tales from mutual friends he kept in touch with, but eventually we both got postcards, then letters, more or less making amends and in a warped way, thanking us.

"It was a call," he wrote, at the end of a long missive kvetching about dead-end auditions, roach-swarmed apartments shared with psychotic strangers, and jobs wearing giant foam foodstuff costumes. "It was a crossroads in our lives. The kind of drama we'd been pursuing all along. And it ended up happening when we least expected or wanted it. She chose you, and for a while I hated you for it. But failure MUST breed opportunity to move forward. I needed to completely disengage to fulfill my destiny."

Part of me thought he was right. The other part wondered if he had joined a cult or had been watching too many episodes of "Oprah."

But he really had changed. He kept at it, pursuing his acting career through hundreds of auditions, hundreds of rejections and countless meals of ramen and hoarded condiments. And after we'd made our peace, throughout the trek, he kept in touch. Maybe it was only to remind him of what drove him out there in the first place. Maybe it was to rub it in that while we were settling into typical lives he was still living the exotic. But he kept in touch. Even up through his first commercial, as a skateboarder extremely enthusiastic about a new orange drink, we had a subscription to the colorful "Moochie newsletter."

However, as his imdb database entry fattened, eventually our subscription expired. Christmas cards were returned to sender unopened, old phone numbers were discovered to be disconnected and Moochie became a fond flashback; worth a smile when he would pop up as an "expert scientist" on an infomercial or as a hit-and-run victim on a medical drama.

Mistri and I took the paths most taken, and it made all the difference. I got into advertising. She works in one of those nebulous business jobs I can never quite remember the specifics of, but which I know has some resemblance to all the Dilbert strips taped up around her apartment.

We both moved to the city and remained friends, occasionally hooking up during dry seasons in the romance department, but spending most of our time trying to fool ourselves into thinking we're vibrant characters in a romantic comedy of our own making. It enlivens and distracts us, although sometimes not quite as much as the evening soap operas we use to get through the more brutally banal stretches.

MLK morning, we chatted and fast-forwarded through our respective tapes of Moochie's big debut, as the "hip, young, new Pope who may just know the true resting place of the Holy Grail," according to TV Guide.

We decided to meet at La Flama Casa that night for cheap, strong Margaritas and enchiladas with an inevitable side order of regrets and self-examination. Once there we slipped into our familiar roles as drunk and drunker, with her verbalizing parallels to what I was thinking but hadn't imbibed enough to express. Vibrant images of coulda, woulda, shoulda beens that we secretly hoped were taking place for us in some alternate reality with such vitality that shockwaves would spread from them, ripple throughout our lives and slowly, but inexorably, draw us nearer to our manifest destiny.

Segueing out of a story about a tragic prom date that had been told with subtle variations close to three dozen times, she told me about an answering machine message tape she pretended to have just found, but which I guessed she had been cherishing among high school pictures and love letters for quite a while. It was from a few years out of college, during the time Moochie was a regular correspondent.

When we got back to her place, she played it for me, fast forwarding beyond a diatribe from another ex-boyfriend begging to get her back and a few strange but amusing blips from her nerdy brother. Just past a "Happy Birthday" call from her three-year-old niece was that familiar, dusty voice.

"Hi, uh, yeah, this is Mike Mancuso," he chuckled, "I just found this number in my jacket. I was wondering if you were by any chance the lawyer I talked to about helping me get custody of my Cuban foster children from my HIV-positive ex-boyfriend?" Laugh. Click.

"You know, we could probably get some bucks from `A Current Affair' for that tape," Mistri slurred, smiling.

Hours later, after a brief, awkward exchange of bodily fluids and a boring, repetitive exchange of insecurities and doubts afterwards, Mistri passed out and I left, hoping I wouldn't be too hung over for work Tuesday.

In the light of a full moon, steady blankets of mayflies smashed against my window in slow motion. It was like driving on the highway during the tail end of a snowstorm.

When I got home, I passed a rusty easel and my tool box brimmed with ancient, squeezed up paints and frizzed brushes. I walked over the cheap, ugly rug drabbed by footprints and time, but still red and vital in reminiscences.

I remembered feeling awful for Moochie that junior year, but also jubilant, having Mistri to myself, even by default. However, it turned out we did help him, by giving him no reason to stay.

And now, perhaps he was returning the favor, in a way. Maybe his success was my own "call," as he put it -- something to smack me in the ass like a rolled, wet towel, to wake me up from my taupe, IKEAed existence. Maybe this was the turning point, to show me what I could've done, should've done, with my life. Perhaps this was the seed that would bloom with me walking away from my job and pursuing something trendy, cool and entrepreneurial. Or at least something that would get me laid easier in the coffee shops.

Or maybe it was just a trivial brush with fame, several times removed, which I could use at a party, to spin into a conversation on the vagaries of luck and chance.

Screw it. I could ponder and stew tomorrow.

It was late. My alarm would be blaring before I knew it, prodding me into another clock-punching day. And my comfortable bed was calling my name, promising me another night of Jennifer Aniston and a good hand.

every number is lucky to someone

Learning To Read

"We'll be fine," I replied to the question unasked, but implied by the odd look in Marisol's eyes. "You go ahead, we'll meet you later."

The call had come at the onset of "family day." The one time a week when work was banned, housework was shrugged off and everything aside our unit of three was ignored.

Usually.

We were halfway into lunch when her cell phone rang, dipping her into awkward euphemisms at the table and finally taking her to hushed conversation away from it.

"Julie," she said, putting her finger over the phone mic before she moved away, and really that was all that needed to be said.

In the meantime, with Mom away, Aaron and I had made the most of the situation. We polished off the lukewarm pizza and played a game we called ``werewolf fangs,'' where the craggy, discarded crusts were placed just under our upper lips to simulate the game's namesake. Although in his case, most often the crusts were hanging precariously from his mouth, it hardly mattered. The sole object seemed to be me acting like a complete goofball to make him laugh.

Lycanthropic possibilities exhausted, I changed out a five to arm myself with quarters for a forklift booth bursting with stuffed animals.

``Get the bike, Daddy! Get the bike!'' He nodded his unruly blond head over his red-and-white striped sailor polo and placed his pudgy paws on the game's counter, next to the joystick.

``I'll give it a try, buddy. Daddy's not the greatest in the world at this game.''

Three dollars and a dozen attempts in, Marisol returned from outside, harried, lightly sweating, her pale skin flushed dark pink and the ends of her auburn hair stained dark and frizzy.

``What's up?'' I said, never breaking my gaze from the metallic arm.

She shook her head and exhaled, exasperated, opening her mouth to speak and then stopping, as if she didn't know what to say. As she stepped closer, Aaron scrunched his nose. She smelled like an ashtray.

``I thought you'd quit?" I said, pushing the button on the joystick. The metal arm gently grabbed ahold of the toy we'd been seeking and finally took hold, lifting it from the morass of plush.

``Yaaaaaay!" Aaron burst out, watching the clamp loosely lofting the red plush motorbike to drop over the exit square on the machine.

``I know," she said. ``I did. I will. I know it's not good for him. I've just been under a lot of stress lately. Work, every-thing, and the whole Julie situation has just been driving me nuts."

``Don't worry, the trip will do us good," I said, smiling at her and then fishing the toy out of the game's slot and handing it to Aaron, who immediately ran to our table to play with it.

``Yeah," she sighed.

One of the main reasons we'd come to the mall in the first place was to make the latest payment on our vacation. A trip for three to Mexico. Aaron's first extended trek away from town. My first extended time away with Marisol since we'd started dating two years ago.

The initial plan was that it was going to be just the two of us. But when two family babysitters -- one being the aforemen-tioned Julie -- proved to be unavailable we succumbed to the wheels of fate and started planning on taking Aaron along. He didn't quite grasp what we were doing, and it needed some explaining to him, but once he latched onto the idea of us going to the country where tacos were invented, he found it to be very exciting.

``So what's up?'' I said, as we watched the boy from a safe distance.

``Oh, the usual,'' she said, looking down at her feet and scraping the bottom of her sole against the tile floor. ``She's, uhhh . . . things aren't going well again.''

``Issues with Tom.''

``Yeah.''

``That sucks.''

She looked up. ``Do you mind if I go over there?''

``No, I guess not,'' I said. ``We'll miss you. We haven't seen you much lately.''

``I know. I'll make it up to you. When everything is okay with Julie. Alright?''

``That's fine. I understand. I'm just worried about the little guy.''

``I know,'' she trailed off, looking at him. ``He enjoys being with you though. You guys have a good time together.''

``Yeah,'' I said. ``Don't worry about us. We'll be okay.''

And we would be. We always were. Especially over the last few months, as we became more of a duo than a trio. But I couldn't be too angry. Julie was rarely okay lately, from what I could tell. Since late spring, Marisol and her once-estranged sister had been nearly inseparable. Late nights, after work, weekends, the calls would constantly arrive. Always on the cell, always with some frantic reason for Marisol to leave us behind.

I was kept out of the loop for the most part. From what Marisol said, and from the uncomfortable vibe I got from Julie when I gently offered any help I could, I got the feeling she didn't feel steady with many people knowing what was happening. That was fine with me. I could respect her privacy.

Still, I started to feel odd about it a few weeks ago. Some things just weren't adding up. Details, things mentioned in Julie's presence, things mentioned by Julie, that seemed incongruous with previous events, spurred me to ask Marisol if she was being completely honest with me.

About a month back, at the end of what began as a potentially dangerous talk, Marisol, after swearing me to silence, told me about the abuse. And everything changed. Suspicions and accusations turned into guilt and a willingness on my part to do what needed to be done.

If this meant more time solo with Aaron, so be it. Not that I minded. Quite the contrary. But I did feel bad for her, missing out on what had been a quicksilver formative time for him, an era of new words and phrases, new foods and games, first rhymes and songs.

At the table again, she put her hand on Aaron's back and kissed him on the top of the head.

``I'll be back before dinner. Reservation is at five, right? Jungle Bungle?''

``Yeah,'' I said. ``Just meet us there. Tell Julie she's welcome, and to bring the kids too if she wants.''

``Sure,'' she said, looking at me with wide eyes that grew glassy for just a second. ``I'll see you later.''

She leaned over and gave me a quick peck, then turned to the boy, running his hands over the silver material approximating a windshield on his new stuffed bike.

``Bye, Aaron,'' she said, leaning over to kiss him again as he turned his chubby cheek from her slightly.

``Bye, Mommy.''

``I know, it was supposed to be our day,'' she started.

I touched her hand.

``We'll be fine. Tell her I said `hi,' and not to worry, everything is going to be alright.''

She nodded, then turned and walked away. Her tall, thin frame faded into a dark blob against the light streaming in through the glass doors. It gained definition again passing to the outside, as she reached into her purse and pulled out her cell phone before disappearing around the corner.

``Why does Mommy always have to go?'' Aaron asked, still looking down at the bike.

``Well, buddy, Aunt Julie has been unhappy lately and Mommy is helping her cheer up. You know That's important, right? Helping other people?''

``Yeah.''

``Someday you'll have a little brother or sister and when they're feeling sad you'll get to help them too.''

``Okay.''

He really couldn't understand, but what did I expect? While he was a pretty smart kid, he was just a little under three.

He sat there silent for a time, as I tried to distract him with games, to no avail. I glanced around looking for a way to change the subject. Fortunately, I found one powerful enough to gain his attention.

``You know, all this talking is making me hungry again. I think I might need some ice cream.''

``Ice cream?''

``Yeah, ice cream. Do you want some ice cream?''

``Uh huh.''

``Okay, but you've got to promise me something.''

``Uh huh.'' His eyes were in high beam mode, panning over to the counter.

``Promise you'll be nice to Mommy when she gets back, okay?''

``Okay.''

``Mommy is being very helpful to Aunt Julie. I know you miss her. I do too. But what she's doing is very important. Okay?''

``Okay.''

Two incredibly sloppy sundaes and five minutes of clean-up later, we left to explore the rest of the mall. We had roughly four hours to kill before meeting Marisol, and with the temperature blazing over 100, an air conditioned enclosure filled with visual stimuli was as good a place as any to pass the time.

It had been a while since I'd really walked around a mall. Most of the time my visits were in and out, zipping into an anchor store to shop or a restaurant to get some food, beeline to one or two other spots and then leaving, on to the next thing on the Sunday "honey do" list.

During my pre-teen and early teen years, this was my haunt. An exotic village with endless possibilities.

Video games.

Batting cages.

Photo booths.

Miniature golf.

Movies.

The bookstore, where my friends and I would sneak peeks at the Playboys on the top shelves when the grizzly, snub-nosed clerk wasn't looking. Having snuck them from the pinnacle of the magazine stand, we'd hide them in the middle of open Sports Illustrateds to get a longer look at the tanned, air-brushed maps of the new world we'd just discovered.

The food court, where three large boxes of fries could fuel an hour of gawking at wandering gaggles of girls, followed by plotting, conversation and endless speculation on just what it would take to win the hearts of the training bra Venuses we coveted.

Journeying around the mall with four hours to kill and a restless almost three-year-old on your hands was another matter entirely, one which required an intense concentration.

The bookstore, minus leering at the top shelf, was a must. Time tore by when it was spent playing with Paddington bears and reading Elmo books while sitting in beanbag chairs on a kaleidoscope rug.

Watching Aaron read, or at least attempt to, was one of the joys of my life. Seeing him glance intently at the pages, his lips open and barely, sorta moving along, his big sky blue eyes darting from space to space, eating up new information, was magical. At home, I would follow along, helping him shape the syllables, place the words. Being there as these formerly intimidating, alien symbols were tamed and transformed into keys to a once-secret universe was one of my favorite activities.

But in public it was quite different. He exerted his independence, wanting Daddy nearby but not too close.

``Me do it meself,'' he would say.

And he would, in his own way. Recognizing a few of the familiar items in the pictures and making up the rest to his satisfaction. Putting the pieces together slowly but surely, while giving his imagination a workout. Learning to read.

And as I listened to his cobbled stories, more complex and fantastic than the simplistic fables committed to paper before him, a part of me wished that those could remain his view of the tales. A part of me was sad about him losing those improvised wonderments once he gained knowledge, once he was conditioned to see what those sentences meant, their alignment defining reality rather than merely acting as a framework to what he wanted to see.

About an hour later, with a small plastic tote of three tomes in tow, he took my hand as we walked out into the mall, sharing a mushy, sickly sweet vanilla ice drink masquerading as something to do with coffee. The Lite Brite-colored mini-amusement park in the center of the mall was our next destination. With its softly bucking broncos, saddles at arms' height, miniature cars and a strange polar-bear-shaped bus, it was a haven for small children and their parents, always ready with more quarters to buy themselves some more time.

Like me, Aaron was always drawn to the polar bear off to the left side, near the chipped, blue Etch-A-Sketch photo booth. The bizarre, icy fiberglass layered shiny, powder blue - and-ivory hair around the bear's chassis. Its body was solid and enveloping, with cracking, burgundy leather seats trimmed in a fingerprint-smudged gold.

Thick paws at the fore and shank, it had serene, dark blue glass eyes and a sweet smile on its face that was comforting. But its incongruity -- a half-animal, half-machine in the midst of several more traditional vehicles (albeit machines with human characteristics like smiley grills and cartoon eye head-lights) -- made it stand apart.

I put him aboard it, strapped him in with the flimsy seat belt, dumped a handful of quarters into the slot and watched him smile as the bear's voice said ``all aboard!'' and it began to slowly lurch and chug.

``He looks just like you,'' a tan, dark-haired twentysome-thing woman in stylish clothes and thin gold necklace and ankle bracelet said to me, as I stood back from the ride.

``Thanks,'' I said. And he did. Tousled blonde hair, blue eyes, a little sun giving him some color, sturdy build.

He wasn't my biological son. I had only started dating Marisol when he was nine months old. But he was my boy. At least I thought of him that way. And when I looked at Marisol, with her pale skin and burnt sienna hair, and thought of his ``real dad,'' Mike, all short, dark and swarthy, I wondered if there hadn't been some sort of weird physiological transference taking place in which he inherited some of my genes through close proximity and emotional contact.

``You seem to really get along well.''

``He's a fun little guy to hang out with,'' I said, glancing back at Aaron waving to me.

``It's nice to have a Dad who takes time out to play with

his kids," she added, with a long look at me and then a quick one back at her children on the taxicab ride.

``Yeah, I guess it is,'' I said, smiling and watching Aaron push on a red button in front of him to clink a bell in the bear's red hat.

At that point, a girl who was obviously the tanned woman's daughter jumped off the ride and came running towards her. She was a tall child of about five or six, with immaculate brown hair, a kitten's-tongue-pink ribbon running through it, and a white cotton dress dancing with thin, frothy pink lines of bears.

``Mommy, can we go to the Skee-Ball now?'' she plead, and her mother nodded.

``The one at Video Game Central?''

``Yeah? What other one is there?'' she gave her Mom a ``duh'' look.

``Well, duty calls,'' the mother said, smiling and winking as she walked away. ``Have fun!''

``I'm sure I will,'' I said, looking back at Aaron pumping his fist and belting out ``Choo! Choo!''

Another child of around eight or nine, part of a pack of three, all chewing large ropes of licorice, jumped on the back of the polar bear ride and jumped off quickly.

``Pee-ewwww!'' the kid said, waving his hand in front of his nose and looking at me. ``I think your kid pooped his pants."

Aaron laughed.

Duty called.

The next stop was one I was sort of dreading, since it would be considerably more complicated. But it had to be done.

The bathroom.

A quick couple of pats on the behind revealed that, at least to this point, the stench was only a warning shot, a harbinger. But I knew it was only a matter of time so we started in the direction of the restrooms.

It's always something of an odd juggling act bringing a small boy into a bathroom with you. No matter how much you love your son, no matter how much you look alike, no matter how much you know it has to be done, there's always that small percentage of you deep inside that wonders if you look like a molester when you enter a stall with a child. It can't be avoided.

And it's especially strained when said child usually insists on singing a song about his ``winky'' as he drops trou and training diaper.

Even more difficult was trying to stand at a urinal, doing your business one handed while your other was kept free to stop the little boy next to you from grabbing and eating the lit-tle ``cake'' in the porcelain trough in front of him at the adja-cent urinal.

Unfortunately, that would be the least of my worries on this trip.

By the time we'd gotten into the long hallway leading to the men's restrooms it was obvious I was too late. A growing stain was forming in the seat of his jeans, one that defiantly spread out above and below the diaper lines and darkened the yellow tractor on his back pocket.

``Uh oh,'' Aaron said as a rocket sound boomed in his pants.

I couldn't have put it better myself.

Getting him onto the too-small diaper changing shelf in the bathroom, I soon realized how dire the situation was. To put it discreetly, the diaper stood no chance against an onslaught I would later theorize to be dairy-fueled. His pants and shirt were the casualties of his digestive war and a large part of his lower back and legs were covered in a creeping goo that smelled worse than anything I'd had the displeasure to experience in my life up to that point.

There was only one way out of this, and it was not going to be pretty.

In the side pockets of my khaki cargo shorts I was always prepared with three spare diapers for a trip this long. The first had been used before we got the pizza and was currently aromating in the bathroom garbage. The second was on him for all of a minute as I started soaking his clothes in the sink when his next salvos splattered forth in quick defiance of my handiwork. I was down to my last bullet. I had to think fast.

---

every number is lucky to someone

Leaving Aaron's shirt and pants soaking in the sink, I tore off a long skein of paper towels and doused them in soap and water. Whipping the defiled diaper off him and chucking it in the trash can, I did a quick wipe with the towels, threw them away and carried my now-buck naked companion into the far stall.

I reached for the seat liners. Out. Reached for the toilet paper. Out.

``Stay here Aaron. Stay right here.''

He stood there naked and laughing as I lurched out the door and into the next stall, which was, thankfully, unoccupied. Three rolls of paper, two of them stripped to the cardboard. The third, paydirt. I whirled it around, collecting as much as I could.

``Winky! Winky! Winky!'' Aaron danced around the stall, cupping his boyhood in his hand.

A scarecrow-thin teenager with red, moppish hair and braces walked in, gave us a strange look, took one whiff and made a beeline for the urinal, pulling his shirt up over his nose as an impromptu gas mask.

Brandishing a gigantic bouquet of unrolled toilet paper, I bounded back towards Aaron's stall. Too late. Seconds too late. It was like one of those slow motion sequences in a Bruce Willis movie where he dives to stop the bullets from hitting their target, a deep ``Noooooooooo'' tragically draining from his maw.

``Uh oh,'' Aaron said, as he inadvertently decorated the

floor and wall of the stall like a Jackson Pollock painting.

Not taking any chances, I rushed to wipe off the toilet seat and put down a thin ring of paper. Grabbing him, I set him down on there. As he'd been instructed at home, as part of his ongoing training, he grasped ahold of the side to avoid falling in. Just in time. He giggled as the next round fortunately hit its proper mark.

``Poop! Poop!" he said, as I jetted out to grab more paper towels for the massive clean-up.

``Stay right there, Aaron."

With at least one rainforest bunched in both hands, I closed the stall door behind me and got to work sopping up the mess. Seeing me pulling my t-shirt up over my nose in a useless attempt to block the ripe aroma made Aaron explode in laughter.

``Daddy, you look funny!"

``Stay there, Aaron."

``Daddy looks funny!"

Fortunately, throughout my toxic waste duty, he remained hunched over, doing his business, which amused him to no end.

``Poop!"

``Poop!"

``Poop!"

With each shower into the basin he added his own unique color commentary.

``Thanks for the update, buddy,'' I said, scrubbing the pink tiled walls.

I didn't keep exact track, but at least a half-dozen other people came and left the bathroom during that time, as I piled up paper, making regular deposits into the tank under Aaron, flushing it down and going back for another round.

With only one diaper left and the closest store carrying them the big box down the road from the mall, I had no choice but to wait it out. Keep him there until the storm had abated.

``Stay there, Aaron.''

The last of his graffiti cleaned up, I opened the door and darted toward the sink, to wring out the clothing left there, grab some more towels and attempt to dry it out for the dangerous trek to the store.

But when I lunged to grab it ... it was gone.

A few minutes before, when I was otherwise occupied, I'd barely noticed a round of what sounded like pre-teen kids cackling in between intermittent whispers. With other things on my mind, obviously, I thought little of it.

I should have thought more.

After all, I was that age once. A wild, post-larval savage loose at the mall, bored and looking for trouble. And as much as I was pissed when I saw the empty sink I knew deep down that when I was twelve or thirteen, with a face full of acne and a head full of devious schemes, this was exactly something I would have done.

Momentarily defeated, I slunk back to the stall, where I waited Aaron out. About forty-five minutes later, when he seemed wrung, I washed him up, dried him and carefully put on the last diaper.

``Okay, buddy, we're going on a little ride,'' I said. ``Hold on tight.''

``Where did my clothes go, Daddy?''

``Some bad guys stole them, buddy. We're going to get you new ones.''

He seemed puzzled, but that was better than upset.

Saying a silent prayer, I grabbed him in my arms and we bolted down the hallway, through the mall. A messy-haired grown man looking like a ragamuffin in a drenched, sweaty t-shirt and shorts, carrying a baby with his hair wet and slicked back, wearing only a diaper. We looked like a bad sitcom duo from the White Trash Network. I walked as briskly as I could, my arms wrapped around him to keep him safe and warm, his strong smell of generic liquid soap trailing behind us.

We made it past the bookstore.

We made it past the mini-golf.

We finally made it past the movie theater and to the door.

And then the smell.

My hand instinctively reached down. Nothing.

``Aaron, did you?''

``No poop, Daddy, just toot.''

``Okay, good.''

Car in sight, I clenched my right arm around him as I reached my left hand into my pocket, grabbing the keychain and clicking the remote. The car was open.

Front seat up.

Into the car seat.

Belts fastened. He's in.

Front seat down.

The smell again.

``Aaron?''

``Toot!''

I ran around to the other side. Car door open. In. Start. Quick look back. Clear. Pulled out. Pulled away. Looking frantically to either side, zipping through the parking lot, past the intersection, onto the street, down the street, hit the light.

``Please, please, please . . .''

Green. Past the light.

Uh oh.

``Aaron?''

``Toot!''

Into the turn. To the next light. Green. There is a God.

Onto the straightaway, around the curve, into the home stretch. Parking lot. There's a spot. It's close. Got it. In.

Door open. Front seat up. Belt off. Baby out of his chair. Door closed and locked. Brisk walk through the parking lot. Through the automatic doors, into the store.

``Welcome to SuperMart,'' the lady extends her arm and I grab the flyer. Just in case. Never know when I might need it.

``Aaron?''

``Uhhhh . . .''

This one had some force behind it. I feel something slimy on my forearm and my shirt. I look down. I'm hit. Something, but not much. I wipe off my arm on my shirt. Nothing compared to the rest. Maybe he's hit a lull. Maybe he's drained. Hopefully.

``Try to hold it Aaron. We're almost there.''

Make it to the kids department and grab the first shirt and shorts I see in his size. Haul a pack of diapers off the shelf and stuff them under my arm. Grab a pack of baby wipes and do the same.

An older lady with fat, square glasses, teal eye-shadow slathered above raccoon eyes, salami-colored skin, boobs to her knees and a paunch that looks like a bowling ball under her Lynyrd Skynyrd tank top gives me a look to maim. A dishwater blonde teen with an inch of dark brown roots, acid-wash jean shorts sliced up to her ass curve and not not quite covering her ass crack, a hot pink tube top and fresh bruises down her pale right arm chomps her gum in my direction.

``Mister you gotta git that there baby some clothes."

``Thanks for the tip."

I get a quick look at myself in a mirror by the dressing room. Red-faced, scarecrow hair, shirt doused in sweat and painted down the middle with reek, cradling a stained diaper baby in one arm and a pack of dipes, a pack of wipes, a pair of My First Budweiser shorts and a tiny t-shirt that says, ``My Daddy Gits Er Dunn!" under my other.

``Daddy . . ."

``Just a few more seconds, Aaron. Hold on just a few more seconds."

On the way to the register, I pass by the men's department and sift through a rack of black t-shirts. The first large I see I lift to add to my burden, then put back down. I don't care how desperate I am, I'm not buying a shirt that says, ``Free Mammograms! Sign Up Here" with an arrow pointing down-ward.

Then I hear it.

Damn!

``Aaron?''

``Toot!''

I grab the next large I see. It's got a girl's dark, smiling face silk-screened on it. She's winking under palm fronds over her head. Next to her is the slogan, ``Get Lei'ed in Hawaii!''

We zoom into the express lane. A middle-aged woman in a striped shirt takes one look at me and steps aside, putting her items back into her basket.

``You can go ahead of me,'' she says, her face pursed in disgust.

The cashier raises her eyebrows as I dump my clothing and diapers on the counter and she whisks it with as little finger contact possible over the barcode-reader and into plastic bags.

``We're almost home free, buddy. Just hold on. Just hold on.''

Chomping her gum condescendingly, she clicks a red button with long, fake, bedazzled fingernails and spews me a total. I whisk my card, sign, get my receipt, put it away with my card in my pocket, grab the bags and breathe out heavily. Only fifty feet away from the washroom and our salvation.

``Daddy?''

``Aaron . . .''

Oh no.

And now it becomes a sprint, the bags flailing around my arms, the boy gritting his teeth and concentrating, trying to keep it all inside, and thankfully, at least doing so until we get into the bathroom, into a stall. Again. The door not closed yet, but yup, at least inside a foot or two when he turns into a little sprinkler.

Another hour of waiting later and we seem to be fine. From the looks of things he's gotten it all out. We've gone a whole twenty minutes without an incident and even the warning shots have dissipated, a hopeful omen of things to come. Or, not to.

Just to be sure, I leave him there, hanging on, singing a song he learned from a big green muppet, as I clean myself up, attempt to make myself look somewhat presentable in my brand new t-shirt.

I don't make the same mistake. Instead, I commandeer the sink area, with my old shirt soaking in one basin as I wash Aaron off in the other. Likewise, I take off the new shirt and hang it over the paper towel dispenser, to avoid getting it drenched with the inevitable splashing.

An employee walks in. He takes one disinterested look at the shirtless man bathing the naked child and attends to his own business, sauntering out whistling without washing his hands. I get the feeling he's seen this before.

With Aaron finally clean and ready to go, I pick him up in

one arm, my bags draped over the other, and beat a path to the door, avoiding any eye contact all the way to the car, where I strap him in without event. We're ten minutes early when we get to Jungle Bungle and walk inside. I check my cell phone. No calls.

Twenty-five minutes later, Marisol arrives. She breezes in on an invisible but unmistakable cloud of nicotine residue, bobbing her head and muttering vague exasperations about her sister. Aaron is playing in a netted cage full of multi-colored plastic balls with three other kids, but nonetheless, in the midst of his reverie, he notices her immediately. He leaves the play area and toddles over to her for a hug.

``What's he wearing?'' she looks at me. ``Wait, what are you wearing?''

``It's a long story.''

``Did you and Daddy go shopping?''

``Yeah, we went to Super-Mart.''

``That sounds fun.''

``Uh huh.''

She glances at me. ``So, did you make the payment, for the trip?''

``Oh, man,'' I slump down into a chair. ``I totally forgot!''

``Geez, Nick, what . . .''

``Don't worry, I'll do it tomorrow.''

``Are they still open tomorrow?''

``Yeah, they should be. I'll take it then.''

``Fine, I guess,'' she exhaled pointedly and sat down, pouring herself a glass of soda from the pitcher.

``So, other than that, everything was fine?''

I look down at Aaron, happily sipping 7-Up from a purple-and-white striped straw, his chubby little arms drowning in an oversized t-shirt.

``My Daddy Gits Er Dunn!''

``Yeah,'' I said. ``It's all good.''

every number is lucky to someone

The Last Cheap Picture Show

``You got any-a-them glory holes?''

This was a question I didn't get very often. I mean, sure, I work in a theater. And yeah, some of the R- and NC-17-rated films we show are a bit on the racy side. But the movie we were featuring tonight was ``Mighty Morphin Power Rangers 5.''

``No, sorry,'' I told the old man in the long coat. ``We only have those open for Disney pictures.''

``Really?''

``Yeah, you should've seen the line after `The Little Mermaid.'''

``Oh, I can imagine.''

He laughed. Well, sort of laughed. More like he began to laugh and then started hacking up a lung. I wasn't sure if he was serious in his pursuit of anonymous prostitution and he was too preoccupied with attempting to breathe for me to ask him. And quite frankly, I just really didn't want to know.

I was in the middle of a profoundly fascinating article in Us Magazine about Jennifer Lopez's ass when he distracted me, and now he wouldn't leave, ogling some of the other reading material I had on a table behind the counter.

``Is that a Penthouse?'' His eyes plead.

Fifteen bucks and three magazines later, he shuffled over to the concession stand. He looked intently, squeezing his rubbery face and sandpapering his hands as he rubbed them against the bristle on his chin and cheeks, probably trying to shave the hair on his palms.

He looked like most of the older guys you try not to notice when you walk through the city -- oddly shaped chunk of white hair, clothes that make him look like he's slowly melting away and a face like a catcher's mitt. There was something both sad and funny about him, like one of those crying clown paintings.

He seemed likely to say something amusing any second, so I didn't mind getting off my duff to get him what he wanted. Sno-Caps, large popcorn, red licorice and a ``big'' Pepsi.

``What size is `big?'''

``You know, that big one over there.'' He pointed his finger over at four cups, none of which was exactly dainty. I gave him the largest one.

``So why were you asking me if we had glory holes?''

``I think that girl Power Ranger looks hot in her tight costume.''

``Yeah, but she's wearing some weird Japanimation mask.''

``So? That turns me on. Makes me tight in the pants.''

This is the kind of information that would haunt me later when I least needed or wanted it to flash its way into my brain.

``It's on the house, buddy.'' I put the final carbonated course of his dinner down on the counter. ``We're closing tomorrow anyway.'' He croaked out a thanks, which kind of sounded like ``screw you'' since he already had shoveled in a handful of popcorn, and shambled away.

``I can't believe you sold that cute little man your smut! You're the manager!'' Leigh was the ticket-taker, a strawberry-blonde nymph with a delightfully lighthearted take on the bad attitude most of us shared.

``Did you see the way he was looking at you?'' I leered. Her face went sour. ``He was licking his lips...''

``EEEEEWWWWW!''

``What's the difference?'' I said. ``He was gonna get it

somewhere. At least this way I made some money on it. Besides, it wasn't my smut. I just found it in the office when I was clearing out the desks. Probably Kenny's. You said he used to always disappear in there for hours."

``I guess. Kind of creepy that he's going to be our last customer."

``Kind of appropriate if you ask me." I looked at my watch. ``Gotta go. Want to join me?"

``Why not?"

Leigh locked the outside doors and we headed up to the projectionist's booth. I had a ``glory hole" of my own to attend to, where I flashed something a bit more wholesome through a portal that provided a few hours of fantasy and, hopefully, enjoyment for the teeming crowd of four in the audience.

This was the final showing of the night, and, therefore, of the theater. Spooling the frames in sequence and looking at the little pictures on them, I couldn't help but have mixed feelings. This was a crummy job, but it was mine for the last two years. It was something to call my own and in its own slacker way it had a certain cache of semi-glamourous underachievement.

This wasn't the life I dreamed up for myself when I graduated college. But with a degree that had given me heavy debt and light employment prospects, I had little choice but to return to the place I swore I would never work again when I graduated high school. I thought that from then on, I was building for the future.

Unfortunately, I must've used Legos by mistake. I expected a ``Friends''-like existence upon graduation, but my life was more like ``Good Times.'' My English degree got me nowhere and with creditors threatening to sell me into an Asian sex ring to recoup at least a portion of their investment, I had no choice but to go for the silver ring -- of a film canister.

However, tomorrow I'll be back to where I once belonged -- unemployed and soon to be living with my parents.

I just hope they have a place cleared on their living room wall where I can hang my diploma.

I remember the first time I ever saw a movie here -- back in the days when the grunge flowed like water and the world hadn't yet known the word Lewinsky. I was going to see ``Reality Bites,'' a movie that certainly lived up to its name. In the ticket booth, a young man cultivating what appeared to be chia on his face looked up from his periodical with ennui and grumbled, ``Yeah, whatta you want?''

Imagine his shock when I announced I was seeking a movie ticket!

And imagine my shock when, a few months later, I was that guy.

Name a theater cliche and I saw it. People smoking. Talking on their cell phones. Bringing alcohol into the venue and sloppily giggling as their empty bottles clattered to the floor. Check. Check. Check.

There were also plenty of people loudly talking or yelling

-- to the people next to them, to the people across the theater, and of course, to the people on the screen. Always to the people on the screen.

Not to be forgotten were the children, whose parents were obviously using the theater as an affordable, soda-soaked babysitter. Periodically, unkempt kids would come wandering through theaters like refugees from a modern production of ``Oliver Twist." You could almost hear them pleading with the concession stand, ``Please, sir, more popcorn, please?"

``In a demented way, I'll miss this place." Leigh looked out at the seats.

``Is there any other way?" I took a swig of my ``big" sized drink.

Both of us watched the movie through to the end, injecting our own wise-ass comments, but mostly savoring what we realized might just be one of the easiest days of work either of us might ever have.

``So, what are you going to do now?" she asked, out of some concern for me, but also out of self-interest. She was a junior English major with a transcript less impressive than mine.

``I have no idea." I slumped in my chair. ``Probably collect unemployment for a few months and coast while I look for an editing job. If I can't get one by September, I'll probably look into a mall job."

``Sounds exciting."

``Uh-huh. As much as this isn't exactly what I wanted to do, at least it was paying me decent money for less-than-hard labor.''

``Yeah. Selling pornography doesn't exactly require heavy lifting.''

``Depends on what you're selling. Or lifting.''

She giggled. The last credits were running, and our final customer was still sitting there, waiting for potential bloopers, or maybe just clinging to shelter.

So, this was it, the last cheap picture show. No Cybill Shepherd. No Jeff Bridges. Not even a Peter Bogdanovich. Just me, Leigh and an old man, laughing at people on screen who were making more to appear in this piece of crap than both of us would in our lifetimes.

Leigh and I slunk down the stairs and towards our destiny. At least for tonight. The concession stand.

``Can I have some of this stuff?'' Leigh reached into the concessions pile I was supposed to inventory before boxing and shipping it off to some nebulous home office.

``Yeah, sure, what the hell.'' I decided to help myself as well, and filled a garbage bag full of candy.

``Hey, did you see that old guy leave?''

I hadn't.

Ten minutes later we were calling the ambulance.

``That was disgusting.'' Leigh's face went crinkly. ``I told you you shouldn't have sold him your smut.''

``How was I supposed to know the guy had a bad heart?''

``He was old!''

``Oh, that's a brilliant deduction.''

We ended up getting overtime that night. Not only did the cops and the ambulance crew show up, but they called his next-of-kin, a distant relation who lived up to the term.

``He was a dirty old man,'' she said, clutching the cross around her neck. ``I told him to repent, to save himself, but it was obvious he didn't. And in the end his vices were his downfall.

``The Lord works in mysterious ways.'' She looked heavenward. ``But at least now, this neighborhood will be spared the sin Harry was going to bring into it.''

``What do you mean?''

``Harry owned this theater.'' Leigh and I volleyed glances. ``When our brother Philip died in April Harry got it and the other theaters in the will, along with a sizable chunk of Philip's money. Philip didn't take to me too kindly. Didn't like it when I turned to the Lord. Harry didn't seem to mind though. Thought it was funny for some reason.''

``So he was the one who wanted to shut the theater down?''

``Sort of,'' she said. ``Not really shut it down completely though. Harry was planning on turning it into one of his porno houses. Told me last week. I prayed for him not to, but I couldn't do anything to stop it.''

She looked heavenward. ``But apparently the Lord did.''

``Interesting,'' I said, not really knowing what else to say, and honestly feeling a little creeped out by the whole thing.

This was one of those instances I've lived through a few times before. A moment I would never believe could ever happen if I'd seen it in a movie or something, but that, sure enough, was really happening to me. It was like meeting my high school girlfriend during a trip to France when we both lived in the same smallish Midwestern town. No joke, really happened. Or my grandma and grandpa dying the same day one year apart. Almost down to the same hour. Eerie. Or my college roommate actually being seduced by a horny blonde MILF when he was a pizza delivery guy. True story, I think, since the guy literally swore over a stack of Bibles that it happened. Although if he's the kind of guy who would bang a strange woman over a pepperoni pizza I don't know if I should trust his allegiance to the word of the Lord.

However, what you could trust in was God's sense of humor. These events were the evidence I used in late night debates with my atheist and agnostic friends. Not the spartan efforts of Mother Teresa or the devout extravagances of any church or religion, but coincidence.

Or, to me, seeming coincidence. What I believe in is that, instead, it's an intricate pattern laid out by a supreme being. The greatest producer-writer-director of all, tying up his plot twists with irony and making himself laugh in the process. Life as, sometimes, one hell of an in-joke. Hey, every holy book says we're made in the Lord's image, and by ``we'' wouldn't that also mean the producers of ``The X-Files'' and ``Lost?'' If they can do it, why can't God? Why wouldn't God?

I mean, for all we knew, this was part of an even bigger plot. Tonight Leigh and I would go out for coffee, and perhaps strike up the real sparks of our to-this-point unrequited sexual chemistry, and someday this would be the story we told our grandkids about how it all started. What a tale. ``The Old Man And Some Porn.'' Sounds like Hemingway.

Anyway, as I was stuck in this mental stupor, my future wife was the more pragmatic of the two of us. ``So, now the theater is yours?'' she chimed in.

The old lady shrugged her shoulders and nodded. ``I guess so. I guess it will be. I'm the only survivor in our family and Harry didn't have any heirs.''

``So, in a way, you're kind of our boss?'' I hoped she hadn't seen the bag full of candy.

``Well, yes, Harry told me if he died he would be leaving the theater to me, but I don't know much about running a theater,'' she said, looking at me. ``You're the manager?''

I agreed, sheepishly.

``Well, I guess I'll just leave things in your hands, as long as you think there's still a place in this city for the type of wholesome fare this theater is already showing."

For some reason, visions of the female Power Ranger doing a strip tease -- but leaving the mask on -- pushed their way into my head.

``Status quo shouldn't be a problem," I said.

The police approached her. ``This is all he had on him, m'aam." They handed her a clear plastic bag. A wallet and various knick-knacks shrunk away at the bottom, below the screaming pink magazines.

``Oh!" She turned to us. ``I'm sorry you have to see this, kids."

She took the bag in her hands and daintily removed anything that didn't feature the word ``hot."

``You know, if it wasn't so sad, it would be funny." She threw the bag-o-zines away. ``We talked and talked about this and I tried to get him to change his ways, but he wouldn't budge. Harry kept arguing and arguing that pornography was going to be the only thing that would save this theater. I guess, in a strange way, it has."

And in the background, in a conversation completely unrelated to our own, I heard a cop chuckle.

Must've been coincidence.

every number is lucky to someone

Heroes

I may be a girl.

I may only be 12.

But I still cannot fathom why a 14-year-old boy would think She-Hulk is the sexiest comic book character in history.

Nonetheless, that is what my older brother Simon's friend Alex is arguing right now.

Needless to say, I'm scared.

``She is!'' Alex maintains, waving a cheese fry in his hand for emphasis and amazingly not splattering any of us with its prefab gloop. ``I'm talkin' old school She-Hulk, like way old school. Before she joined the Fantastic Four and put on that stupid costume. Like, before, way back when She-Hulk first came out."

``No way,'' Tark rolls his eyes.

``Seriously dude, think about it,'' Alex says. ``She's pretty much naked. When she used to go all Hulk and stuff, her clothes would rip off her and she'd only be wearing this seductively frayed shirt that would barely cover her. And then when she changed back to human form you could pretty much tell her boobs were about to fall out of the shirt. And her body was ultra-smack. It was really hot. Hot chick in barely there clothes? You can't beat it.''

``Okay, points for almost nudity, but still, no way, man,'' my brother Simon says, taking a sip of his extra-large Mr. Pibb. ``For one thing, she's green. Don't you find that a little weird, that she looks like Marvin the Martian?''

``She's still hot, especially the way she looked when John Byrne drew her.''

Simon leaned forward, incredulous. ``You mean to tell me she's hotter than any of the babes from Gen 13, hotter than Witchblade, hotter than Dark Phoenix or Storm or Emma Frost, or any of the Manga chicks, cripes, even hotter than friggin' Betty and Veronica?''

Betty and Veronica are Simon's picks. Both. Together. In a sandwich, he says. Nice. T.M.I. Talk about a positive influence.

``Yes!'' Alex maintains, chomping into his fries with

authority, as if the matter is closed by the force of his mandible.

``I still kinda like Sailor Moon," Tark adds out-of-the-blue. ``In her little schoolgirl outfit..."

``That's because you're a perv, Tark," I cut him off.

``Why does that make me a pervert?" he says. ``C'mon, Faith, we go to a Catholic school. We've all gone to Catholic schools throughout our lives. Of course I'm gonna dig the uniform."

``I guess. Perv. You're probably like one of those guys that draws fan art of her taking her clothes off and doing obscene things."

``And what if I am?" he laughed.

``Peeerrrrvvv! Pervopolis! Pervy! Pervski!"

``Whatever."

``Whatever yourself, Joshua."

``Don't call me Joshua."

``That's your name, freak."

``You know I hate Joshua. Call me Tark."

``Why?"

``Just do it."

``Okay, Nike."

``Will you two shut the hell up?" Simon interjected.

Joshua, obviously, hated his name. But to me, Tark was even more stupid. Even if it was just shortening his middle name, Tarkanian, so it made some sort of sense, but still -- lame.

At least when asked about their 2-D objects of lust none of them said Dream from The Sandman comic. That's who I'm dressed as today. Darkness and whimsy in all her glory. She's been my fave for a while. To dress up as, to read about, pretty much all Dream all the time for me. I just think she's cool. She's the best me I can think of -- supernatural powers added in, of course.

As for why I'm dressed in this way, as is typically the protocol in these situations -- comic book conventions -- we're all dressed as our favorite characters.

Tark is Rorschach from the Watchmen, although he took off his mask because it was bugging him and he only wears it for pictures. So basically, with his skinny face and big blue eyes and hawk nose and cowlick shock of black hair he looks like Inspector Gadget. And he hates it when we call him that.

Alex is Han Solo. Alex is always Han Solo. Except for the one time when I saw him as Fox Mulder from ``The X-Files," but that was at an ``X-Files" convention. No, wait, sorry, Alex was Alex Krycek. Simon was Fox Mulder. I got to be Dana

Scully, even though I don't look anything like her, other than the pale skin. I just had to wear a red wig. Then again, neither of those guys particularly looked like the people they were imitating either, aside from the costumes. Both of them look like surfers -- tan, tall, wiry, blond, blue-eyed -- although if either of them had a real muscle between them you wouldn't know it. Anyway, at this juncture, at this time, at this event, at this very moment, Simon is not Fox Mulder. He is Indiana Jones.

``I still think She-Hulk's the hottest,'' Alex said. ``You won't convince me otherwise.''

``Whatever, dude,'' is pretty much the consensus around the table.

Yes, these are my friends. And yes, we are at a comic book convention, eating in the cafeteria, waiting to get the signatures of Jeremy Bulloch and Peter Mayhew, better known as the actors who played Boba Fett and Chewbacca, respectively. And yes, we are complete and utter geeks. And yes, we don't care what you think and we're quite happy with it.

These are our lives. These are our loves. We're not harming anyone and we're having a good time. Get over it.

From the time we were young we were into this stuff. Blame it on our older brother Nick, who eventually gave it up for girls and sports, much to our chagrin. But once he introduced me and Simon to comic books, sci-fi, role playing games and the sort, we were hooked. And so were Simon's friends. It was the same thing as when Nick was introduced to George Carlin and Richard Pryor records by our oldest stepbrother Chuck, who disappeared when we were really young and was never heard from again. Nick couldn't stop playing those records...when our parents weren't home, of course.

When we were younger, Simon, Tark (then known as Joshua) and Alex used to fashion crude capes from our parents' curtains, wrap them about themselves and tear around the neighborhood, throwing rocks at cats, knocking over garbage cans and doing various other things that caused their parents to get irate phone calls.

Grounding didn't work. Threats didn't work. So for some reason, the logic of which still escapes me, they assigned Simon to act as my babysitter, thinking that would cramp his style. Instead, it turned me into a tomboy geek.

I'd never really fit in with my friends at school. At almost six feet by the time I hit 10, I was looked on as an Amazon, some mutant from the missile test range. And don't think my oh-so-sensitive classmates didn't remind me of it at every opportunity. My railroad track of braces and the gigantic glasses clumped over my pasty face didn't help. They only made me look a little like Kareem Abdul-Jabbar, a likeness which I was only too happy no one else in my class had noticed. Nothing against Kareem, but that's a nickname I could live without. That's why I also stayed away from basketball and volleyball. Just in case.

The comic book world afforded me something of an escape. A girl my size was looked upon in its domain as a force to be reckoned with. And with every story I read about a female warrior or superhero, my self-esteem grew. If they could be cool, so could I.

Not to mention that hanging around with guys like this didn't make me feel like such a social pariah. In the world of sci-fi, any girl of remote attractiveness, especially one with a lanky body like me, with long dark hair who could pass for Goth, was considered a goddess.

As time went on, I think my brother realized this, which is one of the reasons why he kept me around. It gave his group a sort of cache to have a girl within their ranks. Even if the girl was his sister. Those looking in from the outside didn't need to know that bit of information. And besides, if there was one girl in the group, maybe the other girls at the event would feel more comfortable allowing my brother and his friends to approach them. It was a logical theory, and it couldn't hurt. The lot of them had never had anything approaching a date, unless you count partnering up for science projects.

None of them had mastered that mixture of cruelty and indifference that proved intoxicating to junior high girls. They remained clueless and overeager, squandering attention even in the rare instances they attracted it, obliviously boring co-ed pool party companions -- who, themselves, were invariably fellow nerds -- with long monologues on videogames, the symbolism of ``Battlestar Galactica'' and the subtle nuances of Chris Claremont's significant contributions to the universe of X-Men comics.

My parents couldn't understand it. Things were far simpler in their younger years.

I still remember the one time I overheard my Mother asking our older brother Nick, with concern in her voice, if he thought Simon was gay.

``Well, I just never see him with girls,'' she said. ``He never brings girls home and he spends so much time in his room with his friends, playing those Dungeons and Dragons games. Do you think they're into S&M in those games and that's why they're called Dungeons?''

``He's not gay, Mom,'' Nick said, stifling a laugh. ``He's a geek. There's a big difference.''

``What do you mean?''

``Well, let's put it this way,'' Nick said, ``if he was gay, he'd be avoiding girls. Because he's a geek, the girls avoid him.''

``Oh,'' she said, pausing for a moment to let it sink in. ``Poor Simon.''

``Don't worry, he'll be fine,'' Nick said. ``It might not be until he gets to college, but he'll be fine. He just needs to be in a place where people understand him.''

Indeed.

These gatherings were necessary to our mental health because they were the only places we really fit in with the rest of the untouchables.

The theory of like molecules gravitating inevitably toward one another was proven true with us. Slowly, through repeated treks to comics and record shops, conventions, Dungeons and Dragons nights at the local library and video game emporiums, we began to coagulate into something of a clique of our own, however leper-like our colony may have been considered. But, bonding over our shared misery, we became each others' friends and thankfully discovered we had more in common than our outsider status. We all enjoyed the insular world of reading and the fantastic realms of science-fiction and fantasy. Not a surprise at any stretch. When the real world is intolerable, imagining yourself in anything else is not only a pleasant departure but a prerequisite to survival.

Even if what you imagine yourself to be is an elf magic user with an absurdly high number of hit points.

Within a few months we had developed a web of like beings to communicate with. Strangelings of various ages and developmental deformities from a smattering of schools within our area.

But even within that group, there were still levels of status.

``Hey Faith, there's your boyfriend," Tark elbowed me, pointing to the back of the cafeteria and chuckling.

``Shut up, Joshua." I punched his arm.

Schlepping to a table at the far end, carrying a tray full of food, was a kid one might generously describe as portly.

Okay, he was fat, there was no way around it.

But you had to admire his guts.

Okay, bad choice of word. You had to admire his courage.

Because this guy, all probably two-hundred pounds of him, was crammed into an exact replica red-white-and-blue Captain America outfit. Complete with winged mask and round shield slung behind his ample torso like a backpack, to allow him to carry his food.

And on top of it all, rather than the blond haired, blue eyed Steve Rogers (the secret identity of Cap in the comic books), this gent was Hispanic.

``Didn't you say you thought Captain America was the sexiest?" Tark said. ``There ya go."

I did. I did say he was the sexiest. And he was, to me, at least. Sure, there were cooler characters. Wolverine, for one. Batman. Sandman. Even the Human Torch. But there was something cool about Captain America to me, about the whole idea of him. About a guy who was so pure in his motives, so determined, that he wound up getting himself literally frozen in time, back in the '40s, back in this era of innocence, before being thawed out and reborn again at a later date. An adult who still had that idealism. An adult who still had that fight. It was very appealing to me.

``There's your luuuvaaah!" Tark laughed.

``Yeah, and there's yours," I said, pointing to a tall, muscular man dressed as an even more dominatrix-like version of Dr. Frank N. Furter from ``Rocky Horror Picture Show." Frank sidled up to the condiment bar, grabbing relish packets and stuffing them in the straps of his black leather panties while making an obnoxious show of spraying mustard over a large hot dog on his tray. He and his companion, a stout woman dressed as Riff Raff, made obscene gestures and laughed.

``Keep that mental picture for later, Tark, I know you want both of them.''

The other guys cracked up as Tark stewed.

I looked back at the good Captain as he laid his tray down on the table and poked through a bag he'd had hanging over his arm. Pulling out a sketchpad and a few pencils, he began to draw with his left hand as he slowly, carefully lifted a greasy pizza slice up to his mouth with the right, taking a huge bite.

He let out a deep breath and his torso heaved, the blue spandex of his costume shining in the sun coming in from the picture windows on one side of the café. Ahhh. Smiling, obviously relaxed, pizza in one hand, pencil in another, what looked to be a gigantic plastic bag of comics on the table down from his tray, he seemed perfectly content in this land where even he could be seemingly immune from torture.

Seemingly.

``Aren't you gonna go sit with him?'' Tark laughed.

``I just might,'' I snapped. ``It's better than sitting with you.''

``Cut it out, Tark,'' Simon jumped in.

``Yeah, don't be a dick,'' Alex said. ``That guy's in the same boat as us. He's here at the convention to get away from getting busted on every day. Give the guy a break. Do you want us to start calling you Log Nose here, like everyone else did at Eisenhower?''

``Screw you, Alex,'' Tark said, his head dropping down towards the table. ``Or should I say, `Basket' Case?''

``Leave it alone,'' Simon said. ``Let's just be happy we're away from that crap and enjoy the day and let others enjoy it too.''

``Fair enough,'' Alex said, pausing, before adding. ``But I still think She-Hulk is the sexiest.''

We all laughed.

Three minutes into a conversation about whether or not Ghost Rider was all flames and a skeleton under his suit, or whether there was some kind of body there, I noticed that our live-and-let live outlook hadn't spread to everyone in the cafe.

Sure enough, it didn't take long for the law of the jungle to be enforced even among the runts of the pack. A trio of guys dressed like Stormtroopers and a Darth Vader descended upon Captain America like an Empirical rain cloud, no doubt hurtling insults his way from the look of it.

When Darth's first punch smacked upon the Captain's ample upper arm, the flesh jiggled ferociously. You could hear the laughter from our side of the café when he struck it again, harder, as the Captain kept his face down, looking at his food, obviously hoping that if he ignored them, they would go away.

``Poor dude,'' Simon said.

``Someone should do something," Alex added. ``Where the heck is security?"

I looked around. Security was apparently out to lunch like the rest of us. I glanced at the three guys stuck at our table, like the dozens of others in the café pretending not to notice, then looked back at the onslaught. The hyenas had already started to pick things off the Captain's plate and the Stormtroopers were doffing helmets to eat their stolen Ding Dongs and Ho Hos.

There was nobody around to do anything. There obviously was no security. The workers behind the counter either couldn't see because they were too busy, or couldn't be bothered because they weren't being paid enough to be. And as for the rest of the crowd? Well, let's just say geeks aren't all that good at confrontation.

But I couldn't help myself. Sure, at school I would remain stoic as the insults rained down, holding it in, pushing down my pain until I got home, to the safety of my room, where I could finally cry and let it all out. Finally release all that hurt. Punch my pillows and whale on the punching bag I had in my room and then when I was good and worn out, lay back on my bed, listening to music and reading whatever comics I had left, unopened, from that week.

But here, for some reason, I felt empowered. Maybe it was all the admiring glances I had gotten throughout the day. Maybe it was a soft spot for Captain America. Maybe it was something more. Like the fact that I was probably a good six inches taller than all the guys who were picking on the good Captain. But I couldn't stand by and watch this occur.

``You guys really are a bunch of pussies,'' I said, standing up and beginning to stride with purpose towards the table of misery, leaving my brother and his friends behind.

My stomach leapt around in my chest like the monster in ``Alien.'' My hands sweated streams. My throat stuck and parched. But I kept going. And all the while, all I could keep on thinking was, ``What the heck am I going to say? What line or catch phrase or something could I use to get them to stop, and then if they don't, what am I going to do?'' At the very least, I was hoping that if they started in on me, someone would come to my defense. Someone who wanted to score points with a girl, not to mention someone who didn't want to see a girl get picked on. I hoped.

``Hey, leave him alone!'' I barked, my voice cracking.

They all turned at once, helmets at their sides, revealing acne scarred faces, sweaty, greasy hair and cruel, jagged teeth. There was a pregnant silence in the cafeteria.

``Yeah, and what if we don't?'' Darth Vader finally spoke up. ``What are you gonna do about it, huh?''

He stepped forward and his hands shot into my chest. He actually pushed me. Or he was trying to cop a feel. Probably a little of both, although there wasn't much to cop.

``Huh?'' he said, as the Stormtroopers cackled. ``Huh?''

``Stop, or what?'' he pushed me again. ``Or what?''

``Or this, dickhead!'' The sound came from behind me, as

did the plate of cheese fries, smacking Darth in his red pitted face. With a berserker scream, Alex slammed headfirst into the pile, knocking Darth backward into two of the Stormtroopers and sending all of them careening to the cement floor.

I turned around just in time to see my brother's Mr. Pibb whipping in midair, smacking the remaining Stormtrooper in the neck. My brother always did have terrible aim. But you just don't mess with Mr. Pibb.

At this point, as if on a director's cue, all hell broke loose and the masses began piling up on Darth and his henchmen, food sailing everywhere, costumed characters crashing into each other and sending one another slipping to the floor. Bits of colored plexiglass and cardboard and rubber cracked at the force of the falls, and the wails of despair over the carefully-crafted outfits meeting their doom filled the hall.

Once the melee broke out, it didn't take long for the cafeteria workers and security to finally take notice and break it up -- more likely than not because they wanted to stop the mess they would have to clean up before it got too out of hand. Darth Vader and his pals tried to blame it on my brother and our crew, but, emboldened by their success, the crowd sided with us and all fingers were pointed in the way of the Empire.

The security guards led them out, each of them crying at the defeat and, even more so, at the shabby state of their uniforms. Parents would undeniably be called and punishments would be meted out. Justice would be served. Superman would be proud.

And at the table, Captain America shined, free again.

``That's the first time anyone's ever stood up for me," he said, practically near tears.

We all looked at one another.

`` I think that's the first time we've ever stood up for each other," I said.

Foodless at this point, we all sat down at the table as the Captain shared what was left of his feast with us. We looked at his drawings, which were pretty good, mostly pictures of a lone hero fighting his way diligently through a large mass of foes, sending bodies sailing with powerful punches and kicks.

His name was Hector and he went to Louisa, a school in the town next to ours. He had loved Captain America since he was a kid, in part because he was the earliest superhero he had encountered. His grandmother, who had been the first of his family to make the trip to this country, gave him the comics when he was just learning to read, enthralled by the red-white-and-blue logo. She was the one who had made him the costume, and although he realized it was ill-fitting on him, whenever he went to a convention he knew it would disappoint her if he didn't wear it.

Typically, he was immune to abuse since most of the people around him were of a heavier set. But there were a few times he was hounded, and those would lead to a sabbatical. Not just from the costume, but from the conventions themselves.

``I like the costume," I said. ``I think it takes a lot of courage to wear it."

He swelled with pride.

We spent the rest of the day with Hector. We waited in line for autographs, saw a few sneak previews of comic book films coming out the following summer, checked out some panel discussions with artists and spent plenty of time on artists' row and among the boxes and boxes and boxes of back issues, debating the finer points of our pet galaxies and stepping to the fore to defend our fantastical passions.

At the end of the day, as we were walking through the halls of the convention center, on our way to the parking lot, we saw a familiar sight. The Empire crew. From the looks of things, they were still waiting for their parents. It was not good.

Hanging around near the doors, with a thick-armed, tattooed security guy with a graying beard and reddish pony tail keeping an eye on them, they were a sad, withered cadre. With most of their costumes torn away, they reminded me of Daleks -- emaciated and pitifully vulnerable without their ominous exoskeletons. Concave chests, insect arms and waists that looked minuscule compared to the huge, padded costumes still sheathing their legs.

They shot us glances of fear mingled with anger and disgust. When one of them mouthed some sort of insult and ``scratched his head'' with an upturned middle finger, Alex gritted his teeth, pretended to cock his fist and fake lunged in their direction. It made them flinch, but with a second to compose themselves, then caused them to whip even more poisonous vibes our way.

Hector and I, bringing up the rear of our group, got the most withering stares.

Looking back quickly to make sure the security guy couldn't see, the jerk pretending to be Darth made a quick but unmistakable oinking sound in Hector's direction.

But I didn't let it matter.

The second I heard the sound, the moment I saw Hector start to deflate, noticed his step grow just a fraction heavier, I did the one thing I knew would be guaranteed to raise his spirits and completely demolish theirs.

I reached out and grabbed Hector's hand.

Grasping it back, shocked, he looked back at me, and I gave him a quick peck on the cheek.

Blushing, his huge smile caused his chubby cheeks to burst beyond the constraints of his costume's cowl, sending the wings on the side of his headgear upward at an odd angle. His stride perked up. He was a superhero again.

We looked at each other, matching grins. His paw snugly holding mine, we strolled out the doors, a couple of misfits unfrozen, reborn.

every number is lucky to someone

Every Number Is Lucky
To Someone

William swallowed the last pill,
looked out the kitchen window at the birds
devouring the new heap of seeds in the
feeder, grinned and glanced at his watch.

11:08.

He would wait three more minutes to
call.

He could feel her smiling at him.
``Don't be late,'' he could hear her saying.
``You're always late.''

He wouldn't be. Not this time.
Superstitious or not, it was maybe the last
chance he had.

``It's 11:11,'' she said on their first

---

date, more than forty years ago. ``Make a wish.''

``Huh?''

``It's 11:11,'' she said, rubbing a finger over the face of the clock and silently contemplating her innermost desire for a few seconds. ``It's God's time. It's the time when you're in line with the universe. If you make a wish at 11:11 it has the best chance of coming true.''

He wasn't sure if she was kidding or not. It didn't matter. It was an eccentric detail, part of the infectious joy she exuded, the magic she brought to his life. The ebullience that stood in such stark contrast to his driving, Spartan upbringing, that made him love her all the more. He shook his head and laughed it off, but that day, for the first time, he made a wish. That she would say yes if he asked her to go out with him again.

That night he was one for one. Batting 1.000.

From then on that ritual was part of their tapestry, the shared strangeness understood between a couple that ultimately binds all relationships.

Over the years many more wishes were made and his average dipped a bit under 1.000. No time more than in the past few years. But the early scrapbook days of their lives together were abundant in blessings, seeming requests granted. So he still felt he came out ahead for such little effort, sending a postcard out to the universe and waiting for a response.

The spring air carried the mingled scents of flowerbeds and lilac bushes heaving to life in through the sheer white curtains of the kitchen. The room flooded with the midday sun against the light yellow tiles and golden oak cabinets. It made for a comforting womb if the news was as he suspected it would be. But he couldn't stay here. Not in here. Not where she had collapsed.

Looking down at his watch again, nervously, he filled a large glass with water. He considered the message on the machine and was tempted to listen to it yet again, dissecting the intonation of the nurse's voice for any trace of emotion in her request.

``Hello Mr. Barstow, this is Jeanine from Dr. Calder's office. We have your test results and the doctor would like to speak with you regarding them. If you could give us a call at...''

Give them a call. Is that good? That they just want to talk to him on the phone? Certainly, they wouldn't give bad news over the phone, would they?

Or maybe they just want him to call so he can set up an appointment to talk to the doctor in person? Maybe that's what they would do? That wouldn't be good. In person is no good. It's never any good. It wasn't with Emily. It wouldn't be with him.

Besides, how could he wait? If they had bad news, he would rather just hear it over the line, know right away, rather than having to make the trip to go in and have them talk to him in person, have to dread every moment, have every possible negative scenario, the worst imaginable, run over and over in his head as he was getting ready and driving over. And what if they couldn't see him right away? Would he have to wait days for the result? They couldn't do that. They couldn't make him wait too long. Certainly, if it was something really bad, something life threatening, something that was going to kill him, slowly or quickly, they would have to tell him right away. Especially if it was something that was going to kill him quickly, because it wouldn't be fair if they waited because in waiting he would have even less time to prepare, even less time of awareness, to know that he was living in the last moments of his life.

Maybe even less time than Emily.

He tried not to think about it. He tried not to think about her for a second. Tried.

Cradling the cordless phone in one hand and the full container in the other he strolled towards the sun room to water the jungle of plants spiking up and draping over their pots amidst the bookshelves jammed with thick, colorful tomes.

His eyes teared a bit as he entered the room. The space still carried the musk of his last dog, Gretzky, and stray furs lingered in the creases and crunched folds of its furniture. Mornings, the two of them would relax. William with the papers, his customary science-fiction or spy novel, a pot of tea and a breakfast heavy with fresh herbs and vegetables plucked from the garden on the patio; his thick, jowly Mastiff with a generous bowl of kibble, rice and chicken and a slobbery toy or rawhide bone for dessert.

The tender beast was good company, particularly after Emily had gone, but he was a notorious shedder. No matter how much they had tried to brush him, no matter how often, it didn't seem to matter. And finally, towards the end, when the hard bristles' caresses against his throbbing joints would cause him to droop and whine, no matter how gingerly William attempted to groom him, they surrendered to the mess. Better to have his steadfast companionship in a halo of molting fluff than to sacrifice his comfort for their vanity.

In the weeks after Emily had died, Gretzky was a constant presence at his friend's side. He followed William everywhere around the house, lumbering just behind him, seeming to hang on his every word. William talked to him constantly, telling the dog about how much he missed his wife, detailing every little thing he longed for about her.

The way her laugh crinkled her crow's feet and she would have to dab a tear away if she was laughing really hard. The way she stood, with her hands on her hips, with that determined little girl look when she looked out on the yard every day and considered what she might do in her garden. The way she couldn't help touching him whenever they were near, putting her hand in his or her arm around him, or even playfully tapping him when he said something silly.

Sometimes William's words would sag into soft sobs. He would sit down and the dog would nudge his massive, fuzzy face against his leg. William would begin to pet him and eventually, his heartbeat would become calm, in metronome with the dog's slow, contented breathing.

The two weeks after Emily's funeral, after their other children had flown back across the country to their homes, their oldest son, Nick, had taken up residence in the extra bedroom.

Just to be there, so they could distract each other with baseball statistics and lines from old movies. They went to the games and the race track, took trips to the Chinese restaurant to have food Emily couldn't eat because of her allergy. Always moving, keeping a blur, divorcing themselves from things that would remind them of her. It was a valiant effort, albeit with predictable results.

And there on the floor beside William, every night, in the bed he couldn't avoid, spread out in a large wicker dog bed filled with inviting comforters and sheets, was Gretzky. He would sit upright for William to pet his head as he fell asleep, and then collapse in a happy heap when the man withdrew his arm just before floating into slumber.

It was there, eleven months later, that William first heard Gretzky whine, noticed he was having a hard time standing up on his own. The vet had said this might happen, just as he said that upping the dosage of his pills could end up causing even further damage inside.

It wasn't long after that.

When the time finally came, when he could no longer bear to see his friend being inexorably eclipsed by pain, William called the vet, made the appointment and sadly counted down fourteen days. Those last two weeks were devoted to cultivating and bathing in Gretzky's buoyant, slobbery aura. Long rides with the windows down. Trips to the park. His own dishes of ice cream. An endless supply of fresh rawhides and toys with squeakers that made his ears perk and his eyebrows spread. And while watching TV or reading a book, hours of William running his hands over the velvety fur on the top of

Gretzky's head, the dog's favorite spot, stopping to scratch behind the ears as the Mastiff's eyes slunk half-shut and he panted happily.

In truth it hadn't been measurably different than their lives together since Emily had gone. But it was pursued with a thirst for detail to commit to memory, to allow him to linger on in the ether of William's mind with a more palpable presence beyond his time.

When his day came, William couldn't hold back the tears. When they got to the hospital, he struggled with the decision until he looked again at the X-ray, saw the mass taking his companion over, realized that he couldn't force his boy to endure any longer for his sake.

With William by his side, lovingly rubbing his belly, his favorite spot, the needle went in and Gretzky, for the first time in such a circumstance, didn't flinch.

``Good boy,'' the nurse said, patting his head.

``Yes, he is,'' William said. ``Yes, he is. That's my boy. That's my Gretzky.''

And then, the dog's smile closed, his wet eyes shuttered, and he was gone.

Nick had been waiting for William in the lobby, to take him home. Surprising his father, he had taken his vacation during this time, to spend it with William, the way he had taken leave the year before, when his mother had died. As Nick had correctly figured, the loss had ripped open the still unhealed wound of his mother's death, and his father needed him by his side, at least until he had gotten over the initial wound.

They had talked of getting another dog, a puppy, or perhaps rescuing a stray from the pound, but in the end it was only Nick that ended up going home with three new pets, saving each from the same fate as Gretzky, albeit perhaps before their time.

William chose to remain alone, for the while. Better not to be attached to anything than to lose it, he said. Especially if he were to lose it quickly. That, he couldn't take.

With Emily, as with Gretzky, there hadn't been much time before the end. A trip to the E.R. A battery of tests. No call, no wait, a result after a day in the hospital.

Three weeks left, they said.

Three weeks.

The doctor was amazed she hadn't come in sooner, hadn't complained more about the pain. He marveled that she had been able to keep it down with, as she put it, ``a lot of aspirin and wishes.''

It wouldn't have mattered when they had caught it anyway, he said. She was being devoured and it couldn't have been stopped.

It wasn't fair, William insisted. It wasn't fair. Wasn't fair that forty years would have to be reduced to three weeks. Especially when they had only just retired a few years before, when they had had so many plans, so many adventures, so many things to do, things they had worked for, saved for, strived for, places to go, a world to share.

And then, a cough.

Nothing, she said.

Nothing.

Then she folded to the floor one day with a thud, coughing uncontrollably, splattering the yellow floor of the kitchen with little dark red flecks, with the dog woofing deeply as William sped through 9-1-1, ``come on come on come on'' and the answer and the cry, quickly, quickly, send an ambulance, okay and he dropped the phone and the dog quit woofing and stood sentinel as he dropped to a knee over her and held her hand and told her he loved her and told her to hold on, hold on, hold on until they got here and he could get her to a hospital, and then the bell and the dog woofing and sorry Gretzky and the sunroom door closed with the dog behind it so the strangers could come in with their tubes and their bags and their boxes of things to attach to her as they pulled her up on the big silver tray, pulled her up and out into the back of the truck as William slammed the door shut behind as they strapped her in, and William pulled up into the back with her and them slamming the door shut behind him and speeding off in the direction of the hospital finally getting there and yanking her in and the calls from the people at the desk and in the line with them and getting her into the room and hooking her up and she's fine she's not having an attack but we're going to have to do tests and ``I love you'' and ``I love you too'' and ``I'll see you later honey'' and ``Please don't go'' he said to her feeling bad about being such a fatalist but saying what he couldn't help but feel as it came to his mind, flooding out of him exploding from his heart and her reassuring squeeze of his hand and ``Don't worry I'm not going anywhere'' and a wink and he felt better and she was ready and gone on a chair as they told him to wait a while.

And wait.

And wait.

Phone calls were made, arrangements, requests left with family members. Come by, yes. Could you please do us a favor and stop by to let the dog out and feed him, thanks. And yes, she's going to be fine they said, she's going to be fine.

She's going to be fine.

And then, she's not.

One trip canceled, another one scheduled. And then another. And then a third to another place, when he knew the answer, knew it deep down, but couldn't bear it, couldn't tolerate it, couldn't, until she said it was okay. She said it was time. She said it was going to be the same answer wherever they went, whatever path they took. Three trips taken, none of them expected, none of them lolled over on Sunday afternoons, none of them greeted by a rush of breath and a flush of dreams, planned out in candlelight, their bodies soft against one another on a Saturday night, her snug in his arms, her head on his chest, his fingers stroking her hair, his heart beating distant in her ear.

Three trips, each more manic than the one before.

And the one long discussed, to a foreign land of origin she'd never seen, the one never taken, would never be considered again.

Their remaining journey would be just as memorable, he promised.

Their last night at home, he cooked her favorite dinner for her, chicken cacciatore with extra garlic, as she put the finishing touches on another scrapbook, one detailing all the vacations they had taken together. After a meandering meal and sweet bowls of chocolate gelato and strawberries, they made love and they stayed awake in bed together late into the night, talking. About the first time they met. About their marriage, their children. About a lifetime of laughter echoing back to bring fond smiles and welcome tears.

At the onset of morning she woke suddenly, struggling. She couldn't breathe. A manic call. Another rush. Another trip to the hospital. This time the final one.

He hadn't even gotten the full three weeks with her.

Their waning moments together were spent in a large hospital bed. Her propped up, lying on her back, looking towards him. Him, scrunched on his side, next to her.

``What will I do without you?'' he said to her, holding her hand.

``I'll be with you,'' she said, voice fading. ``I'll be there... waiting for you, as always.''

She laughed weakly but stopped short, going motionless. Silent.

``I love you,'' he said. ``I love you.''

She didn't respond, but he wanted to think that she heard him, that it was the last thing she heard from him.

Then her chest dropped and she became smaller. And the room was filled with the rude whine of the machine and the distant sound of the clattering of hard shoes moving fast against the floor, louder and louder, to the door of her room.

The woman who was his entire life had been taken from him by a growing black hole on an X-ray.

One which had now, perhaps, finally spread its inky grasp out to him.

11:10.

Only one person knew. There was only one he could call and swear to secrecy knowing he would remain silent, optimistic, understanding. Nick. He loved his other children just the same but they had a far more difficult time dealing with tragedy. He loved them too much to string them along, waiting with him, for the results. But he had to tell someone, had to have a confidante, a rock, the only one remaining, and so he turned to Nick.

``They're just tests,'' the son said. ``Things could look exactly the same. It might not have metastasized; you might be exactly the same as you are. So don't get too worried about the whole thing."

``I don't know," William replied. ``I think I might be joining your Mother soon. I just have a feeling, like she's been waiting."

``Well, she always did say you were late for everything."

He laughed.

``Don't worry, everything is going to be fine," Nick said before he got off the phone. ``Either way, everything is going to be fine."

William looked at the clock to see it change. A good omen, he thought.

11:11.

He made his wish.

Then he dialed the hospital.

The nurse answered immediately, pleasantly, and asked him to hold on the line. Just a few seconds, and then the doctor took over, voice stern and matter-of-fact, demeanor hardly encouraging.

The numbers were low, he said, knowing William understood what that would mean.

He gave William more numbers. Elements of time. Quantities of dosage. Qualities of each increment he could seek to stretch and strain against the inevitable. Then, finally, another set of numbers. A day. A time. A room. More tests. Some hope. Some, but as William could tell by the words unsaid and the timbre of the doctor's voice, not much.

The conversation ended on an artificially up note, when both knew they were lying. But they were too polite to say anything about it.

The doctor hung up and the line went dead. William sat there with the phone in his hand until the silence emanating from it turned to brief static, then a captured voice repeated over and over and then to an insistent beep. Another rude push of sound, reminding him of an earlier day.

William stood up, breathed deeply, dropping his arms to his sides and letting the phone fall onto the couch. Far away from the receiver in the other room. He had three more phone calls to make, to his kids, and he knew they would not be easy.

He breathed heavily again, and looked around the room, remembering for a second when and where they had acquired each item. Some memories fast, some slow. For a moment his legs buckled, and he had to sit down, falling onto a chair and feeling the warmth of the soft saltwater down his cheeks.

Gaining himself again, he looked at the clock on the wall.

11:11.

Still.

It had stopped.

The battery had run out.

He laughed until he cried again, breaking down into sob-bing, before collecting himself, his eyes red and raw, thinking about what he would say to the kids.

``Everything is going to be fine,'' Nick had said.

He reached for the phone. It had slid beneath a cushion. When he pulled it out, it was furry with leftover Gretzky hair stuck to it.

``Everything is going to be fine,'' William said, as he cupped it in his hand, seeing for a second his old companion splayed out on the floor, his chewed, defeated toys within paws' reach. He looked outside, saw the figure of his wife, standing above her garden, gloves dirty, pink bandanna in her hair, waving to him and smiling.

He looked again, and they were gone.

``Either way...''

There, he sat, serene, watching the birds outside, chitter-ing among themselves, pecking away at seeds fallen from the trees, strewn about the yard.

``...everything is going to be fine.''

Then he saw them again.

Emily.

Gretzky.

Patiently, happily waiting for him. Under the cool shade of a willow tree. Its branches dancing softly in the early summer breeze.

Everything is going to be fine.

every number is lucky to someone

Previous Books
By Sean Leary

Sean Leary's Greatest Hits
A Collection of Columns 1990-1999
(pop culture columns)

Sean Leary's Greatest Hits, Volume Two
A Decade of Dispatches: Columns 1993-2003
(pop culture columns)

Exorcising Ghosts
(graphic novel)

Your Favorite Band
(screenplay / stageplay)

Dingo Boogaloo
(screenplay / stageplay)

Also a contributing writer
to
The Dingo, issues 1-6

and contributing editor
to
Archangels Reveal The Shocking Truth
Of The Book Of Revelation

don't worry

For more stories
and other writings
see
www.seanleary.com

Breinigsville, PA USA
15 November 2009
227629BV00001B/27/A